THE GUIDING EYES

Michael Till

For my dear wife Gillian,
with love & gratitude.

CONTENTS

PREFACE

11th September 2001

This story took root when the Twin Towers fell; three thousand people were killed and the whole world gasped, then held its breath. Undoubtedly, the serpent that caused the most horrific enemy assault ever known on mainland America was Al Qaeda, and the reputed head of that serpent was Osama bin Laden. Whether or not he had any actual input to this outrage, or merely gave it a nod of approval, we shall probably never know. Cost became no object; the serpent's head had to be severed from its body and the US Department of State put out a reward of $25 million for information leading to the death or capture of the notorious and dangerous OBL.

Intelligence available at the time, led the USA to believe that OBL was in hiding in the mountainous regions of Afghanistan, known as Tora Bora. Countless millions of dollars were spent on US and British military actions and aerial bombings across the whole mountain region. Special forces were deployed

1

to follow up on every reported sighting, but to no avail. The allied armies, air force, CIA and other agencies were thwarted, and the USA in particular was frustrated beyond all reason. The huge reward failed to secure any lead or useful information. Despite the very latest in satellite surveillance, military might and weapons technology, Osama bin Laden avoided capture and stayed one step ahead of his would-be captors.

In March 2003, US and coalition forces invaded and occupied Iraq. Although the fighting only lasted for approximately one month, Saddam Hussein went into hiding for eight or more months. For the invasion to be successful, it was essential for the Iraqi people to see the dictator arrested and brought to justice for his many crimes against his own country. Although they were not linked to each other these two evil fugitives from justice had to be apprehended at all costs...

CHAPTER 1

The telephone was ringing and David answered it on the kitchen extension.

'Hello. David Sorensen speaking.'

'Hello. This is your older brother here.' This always amused David as Francis was, in fact, his only brother.

'Hi, Frank. It's good to hear from you at long last. I never seem to get hold of you whenever I call. You're always out. How are you keeping, are you well?'

He ignored the question. 'Have you ever considered what we are all doing here, David? I mean, what actually is the object of it all?' he asked. His voice sounded low and raspy to David. Maybe too many cigarettes and late nights, he thought.

'I am assuming you're referring to life on Earth, are you? Well, at a rough guess I'd say it was to expand our species. You know, multiply and develop.'

'Oh, really? Well I'm fifty-seven and you'll soon be fifty-four and neither of us have fathered any children and not likely to do so anyway. So where does that leave us in the great scheme of things, eh?' He was always like this, a bit argumentative and opinionated.

'I'm not saying having children is the only object in life,' David replied. 'Developing our civilisation and prosperity, global health and happiness must be considered also, don't you think?' There was a silence on the phone, whilst he was waiting for Frank to say something.

When he did answer he sounded weary. 'Well, who cares, anyway? That's not why I am calling. I need to speak to you, David, you and Jenny, but not on the phone. Can I visit you and stay over for just a couple of nights, say in about two weeks' time? Will that be OK?'

'Absolutely OK. Hell, we haven't seen you in two years. We would love to have you stay, but why wait a couple of weeks? Come sooner if you can.'

'I am finishing off a painting, oils on canvas, and it must be ready to exhibit in Launceston no later than Friday of next week, so I need the time. It's a moody night scene of Paris after rain with glimmering streetlights, wet roads and the Eiffel Tower in the distance. No, two weeks would work fine for me, if you're OK with that.'

'We look forward to seeing you, Frank. Call me later with your train timings and I'll pick you up from the station. By the way, the painting sounds good over the phone. Take a photo of it before you place it, will you? I'd like to see it.'

'That's not the same as seeing it properly. Just so you know, I very rarely go out. I just do not answer the phone. When I am painting, I become totally absorbed and do not like to be distracted. I keep some odd hours too. I will phone you back in a few days. Goodbye.'

With that the line went dead. David went upstairs to give his wife the news. She was in her underwear sitting in front of the bedroom mirror with the hair dryer in her hand. He flopped onto their bed near her and related the conversation with his brother. Jenny stopped the hairdryer for a moment and watched his reflection behind her in the mirror.

'I think something's up, David. That's so unlike Frank, isn't it? We usually have to beg him to come and see us. I don't think he has ever been here at his own suggestion. I can't wait to hear what his news is. Do you think there could be a woman involved?' She smiled.

David shook his head. 'I doubt it very much. Since Pam died, he became so distant from everyone, a real recluse. I don't think he eats properly, either. Seems to get by on cigarettes and booze. He was as skinny as a rake the last time I saw him.'

Frank was always the artistic one in the family and took his painting very seriously but he was not really a commercial success. To make a decent living as an artist your talent must be above a certain line and Frank was just marginally below it. He did sell most of his work but it was hardly a good living. When his wife was alive, she earned good money as an importer of fashionable ladies' clothing for the smaller retail shops, and they seemed to have a good life. However, when Pam died Frank's finances soon declined.

When their father became ill the old man sent for David and, in strictest confidence, they discussed his will regarding the financially insecure older son. David was in full agreement with his father when he suggested that Frank should be the sole benefactor of the family home and that the father's savings would be split evenly between the two brothers. It was not a fortune in cash but the sale of the old house would go a long way to give Frank some security and allow him to continue with his artistic life.

When that day eventually arrived and the solicitor read out the father's will to the two brothers, Frank became upset and embarrassed by the obvious inequality of the father's wishes but David, using great sensitivity and tact, assured his brother that the decision was absolutely fine and acceptable. Not only did he not need the money but it would please him very much to see his brother Frank set up once more in a stable lifestyle. If anything, it brought the two of them closer than ever before emotionally, but Frank would always remain the recluse.

Selling his dad's house and his own apartment, Frank bought a charming little thatched cottage in an isolated Cornish village, 'far from the madding crowd', and immersed himself in his world of art.

After their conversation in the bedroom Jenny suggested that they drive into Kingston upon Thames, primarily to purchase new pillows and bed linen for the spare bedroom prior to Frank's visit. They had a pub lunch just off the market square and finished the day off by taking in a movie at the multi-screen cinema not far from the rail station. The car park fee was more than the price of the cinema, and when they got home Jenny busied herself preparing a light evening meal for them both. David, on the other hand, found his thoughts wandering way back in time when he and Frank were at school. He thought how similar they were in some respects but so different in others. They were both sensitive guys who could easily show empathy and emotion but David was more outgoing than his brother, could mix with people more easily and had a good sense of humour. Frank could be moody and could readily switch off to people around him and he never suffered fools gladly. Despite these small differences David loved his brother and looked forward to seeing him soon.

That night he had the most realistic dream ever. It was like viewing a movie, very clearly, and Frank was the star. He was looking at his brother's lone figure slowly walking in the dark along a narrow country road. There was no footpath of course, quite normal for country lanes, and there were high hedges on both sides. Suddenly a dark vehicle drove quickly around a sweeping bend and hit Frank from behind. David saw the body shoot forward like a rag doll and lie motionless, face down in the road. He was powerless in his dream to do anything but watch.

The driver, a young man dressed smartly in a striped suit, was kneeling by Frank's motionless body and making a phone-call. He had ginger hair and was tall and slim. David saw him go back to his car, which was a large BMW SUV, and switch on the hazard warning lights, then return to Frank's body until police and an ambulance turned up. As the medics attended carefully to his brother the police officer was talking to the BMW driver and then breath-tested him. It was a minor point but it was something that

David remembered; the policeman had a dark beard. As a qualified graphic designer, that sort of detail easily registered in his memory. He then saw Frank being placed into the ambulance on a hard, narrow carrier with handles on each side.

Eventually all three vehicles drove away and David's viewing of the country lane went black. He didn't awaken until the morning but when he did, that dream was vivid in his mind. He kept it to himself until he and Jenny were seated at the kitchen table for breakfast and then he described the dream to her in every detail. Although she listened patiently, she did not show any surprise or amazement.

'Let's face it, David, you were thinking of your brother a lot yesterday, and as he didn't say why he wanted to visit us so soon you might have suspected that it was something sinister. Put all that together and understandably you could have had a nightmare about him. I can accept that could happen, but just remember this, it was only a dream, OK?'

'There's a bit I forgot to tell you, and it makes it all even stranger. I wasn't actually asleep when I had the experience.'

'What? You had this dream while you were awake?' She looked at him, amazed.

'Well, sort of. You know when you are first lying

in bed relaxed, eyes shut and drifting into a kind of slumber, sleepy but still conscious of noises around you, like a car horn outside or the clock in the hall chiming? Well, that's where I was last night when I had the dream.'

'I know what you mean,' she said. 'Some people call that the twilight zone. Go on.'

'OK, as I was in this twilight zone I saw this unusually bright light in front of me which then dimmed a bit and then I saw a pair of eyes, human eyes that is, no face, just the eyes. They got very close to me and then they seemed to merge with me and I appeared to be looking through them at Frank, on the country road.' She watched him mopping up the last of his egg and bacon with a square piece of toast. She knew that he was far from being a fantasist, but this dream of his seemed to have impressed him somehow.

'If this is going to bother you,' she said, 'why not give your brother a ring on some pretext or another and that will put your mind at ease?'

'No. It's OK. He won't answer anyway. He's got that painting to finish and he gets so detached when he's at the easel. It's like you said, Jen. Just a bad dream. Mind you, it was a very vivid one. Anyway, I will be out in the garden should you want me. At long last I am going to demolish that rotten old garden shed of ours. Been meaning to do that for months and now today is the day. We can order that new one we saw online.'

Three hours passed and David reappeared at the back door covered in dust, dirt and cobwebs. Jenny was doing some ironing in the kitchen whilst watching an old movie on the small television set. 'Good grief, David! Look at the state of you! You're filthy.'

'I know,' he laughed. 'It's all down now and broken up ready for the tip but it will take me at least three trips to get rid of it all. Right, I'm going up for a shower and change of clothes.'

She looked at the kitchen clock and saw it was nearly half twelve and considered what to make for lunch. A few minutes later the telephone rang and Jenny answered it.

'Hello, is it possible to speak to Mr. David Sorensen, please?' The caller was a man.

'I'm his wife. Who is calling?'

'I am sorry to trouble you, Mrs. Sorensen. I am Sergeant Gary Long from the Devon and Cornwall Police. I need to find the next of kin to Mr. Francis Sorensen and hoped your husband could help. Is he available please?'

Jenny suddenly went cold and sat down. 'Sorry,

but he's in the shower right now. What do you mean "next of kin"? Has something happened to Frank?' Her voice had gone up by a couple of octaves.

'I will have to speak to your husband later for the record but I am sorry to inform you that Mr. Francis Sorensen was involved in a fatal road accident last night. I'm also sorry that it has taken this time to reach you. We knew who he was from identification that was on his person, but we could not get into his mobile phone, you see, because of the security code. Not last night, anyway. Now that we are in, we can see his address book, and your telephone number is shown under "Little brother David." I am deeply sorry to have to break this news to you, Mrs. Sorensen. May I leave my number with you for your husband to call me back when he is free? I can give all the details then, if that's OK? Just tell him to ask for Sergeant Long.'

'Of course, yes. I'll just get a pen.' Tears stung her eyes and blurred her vision as she scrawled the number across an envelope.

The Inquest

They drove down to Launceston the day before the inquest having first booked a one-night stay at a Travel Lodge. The Coroner's Court was quiet and run in a very orderly way, as one would expect. David and Jenny sat to one side reserved for interested parties and watched intently as evidence was brought before the coroner either in witness or statement form.

The first witness was called and David sat up with a start as a uniformed policeman with a dark beard came into the room. He was exactly as David had visualised in the dream. He never mentioned anything to Jenny who sat next to him, but when the next witness came in he was a tall, smart ginger-haired young man and spoke of driving his BMW car that night, she squeezed David's hand tightly.

They heard how, on that fateful evening, Mr. Francis Sorensen had walked to his local public house where he had consumed a meal and then spent the rest of the evening drinking.

His blood alcohol level was sufficiently high to have made him intoxicated. At approximately ten thirty that evening, wearing a dark overcoat and black woollen hat, he was making his way home along the country lane. Enquiries showed that this was a regular occurrence.

At that time Mr. Steven Hemsworth, an antique dealer from Exeter, was driving back to Devon having made a late evening business transaction in Cornwall.

He maintained that he was not travelling at an excessive speed but he was negotiating a long sweeping bend. By the time he saw Mr. Sorensen, who was dressed in dark clothing in the middle of the country lane, it was too late to avoid him. Mr Hemsworth was breath tested at the scene by police and was found to have no alcohol in his breath.

When the medical report was read out in court it stated that the cause of death was trauma to the spine and head resulting from the collision. He was pronounced dead shortly after arriving at A and E. Also, on his record was shown that he had recently been diagnosed with advanced pancreatic adenocarcinoma, too advanced for surgical intervention.

David and Jenny had lunch in a small restaurant before making their journey back home to Twickenham. Their visit to Cornwall had proved to be a revelation of sensational proportion.

During the drive back towards London they took the opportunity to discuss their thoughts in detail. First there was the bombshell about Frank's terminal cancer, which must have been behind his request to visit them, David being his only living relative. Then there was David's uncanny account of seeing, like a fly on the wall, his brother's death in such accurate detail and at exactly the same time as it was taking place. It was totally beyond the comprehension of them both. At one point Jenny casually asked him, 'Tell me something. As you got into bed that night, were you thinking of Frank? I mean, were you seeing him in your thoughts?'

He thought for a while before answering. 'Well, I guess I was. He had been on my mind quite a bit that day after his phone call. Why do you ask?'

'This strange event of you seeing Frank at that particular time sounds to me as if it was brought on by you. Do you see what I mean? Brought on by you, concentrating on him just prior to going to sleep. Do you want to see if you can repeat the experience by concentrating on someone else just before sleep? Or do you think it only happened because of the close family relationship?'

He thought for a minute and shook his head. 'Not a bloody clue on that one, Jen, but I'm willing to give it a try tonight. I've nothing to lose by trying,'

They drove on in silence for a while, both lost in their own thoughts until eventually Jenny spoke. 'Just a thought, David, but if this peculiar happening was something that you could repeat, then surely you would have to try and do it in normal waking hours, wouldn't you? Otherwise the person you are concentrating upon, would just be asleep also and that wouldn't be any kind of proof that it worked, would it?'

'Yes, you're right. I would obviously need to see the person doing something and then we could check up the next day or so to see if that's what they were actually doing. That is not going to be too easy, is it? I mean, who the hell is going to tell you in detail exactly what they were doing the day before? They will think you're being a real nosey parker!'

She laughed. 'Anyway. We are getting way ahead of ourselves here. It might never happen again, and what happened regarding Frank could just be a one-off phenomenon.'

Except that it was not.

The Experiment

When they got home, Jenny rummaged through a pile of photographs in a drawer and selected one of a woman standing in a large marquee next to a small table with a flower arrangement on it and showed it to David.

'You do not know Helen but she is a friend of mine from the flower arranging club. Her husband has recently left her, usual old story, and she is having a rough time of it, emotionally speaking. Now I know for a fact that she is treating herself to three days at the Foxhills Country Club, that beautiful hotel in Surrey. It's to cheer herself up really and she is going with Denise, a close friend of hers. Today is their first day there. I know this because she said that she would be back in time for our meeting on Friday evening. Study the photo and see if you can pick up anything on either of them while they are at the hotel. What do you think?'

David was hesitant. 'I'm not too happy about this, Jenny. It's nothing more than distant voyeurism. If it does work, and I get to see what they are doing, I think I'll feel as if I am a peeping tom. Can you see what I meant?'

They looked at each other silently for some time until Jenny broke the ice.

'I can fully see how that could happen and I understand how you are feeling. Generally speaking, I would never encourage you to do that, but what if I stayed by your side and you could whisper to me what you were seeing? If I thought it was becoming inappropriate, I could wake you up out of the dream. What do you think about that idea?'

He nodded his approval. 'If you could do that I would feel a whole lot better about it, and safer too. It's nearly seven twenty at the moment, let's give it a go right now shall we?'

He loosened his clothing, removed his shoes and lay back on the settee and studied the photo.

Some minutes went by and he started to feel drowsy. Just as the hall clock struck seven thirty, his eyes closed and in the darkness he saw a thin bar of light approaching him from the distance. It seemed to stop about one metre away from him and the brightness dimmed a bit and he was then looking at a pair of eyes illuminated by a clear green light. Almost imperceptibly, the eyes drew closer to his face, becoming blurred about ten centimetres away then suddenly, *POP!* It was as if he was now looking through them and he was gazing around a large, beautiful dining room. A short distance away from him, seated at a table for two, were two ladies. One he immediately recognised as Helen from the photograph and the other, he guessed, must be her friend. It appeared to David that they had just finished their evening meal, as a waiter was clearing away the empty plates. He heard Helen's friend ask the waiter if he could serve coffee for two in the lounge with two glasses of Southern Comfort also.

As they stood up to make their way to the lounge David watched and took note of what they were wearing. As planned, he managed to whisper to Jenny what he could see. Helen was in a black dress with silver diagonal stripes across the top part and her friend was wearing a dark blue two-piece suit. As they were leaving the dining room, he noticed that Helen was carrying a paperback and when they settled in the lounge, she put it on the table in front of her. He clearly saw that the book was entitled 'The Girl who Played with Fire' and the author was Stieg Larsson. At this point, only a few minutes into the viewing, David stopped his commentary and fell silent. Jenny looked at him closely and could see that he had gone into an ordinary sleep state. She took the opportunity to slip out into the kitchen and put a frozen baguette into the oven to warm up and started preparing something for their supper. She would let David sleep for a little while as he must be tired after the long drive back from Cornwall.

At the Friday flower club meeting Jenny made a point of asking Helen about her break at the four-star hotel in Surrey. She absolutely loved it and spoke about the wonderful surroundings, the grounds, the spa and dining rooms. She told Jenny that the break had lifted her spirits a bit and they had enjoyed the spa facilities, with its sauna and lovely swimming pool.

She showed Jenny a picture on her mobile phone of her friend Denise and herself that she had asked the waiter to take for them. They were seated in a sumptuous lounge in armchairs with coffee cups and liqueur glasses in front of them. Jenny noticed from the picture that Helen was wearing a black dress with silver diagonal stripes across the top part and on the table in front of her was a book called 'The Girl who Played with Fire.'

As the weeks passed by, they regularly tested David's new-found ability, mainly on well-known performers. For example, if they knew beforehand that a particular singer or band was performing live at some venue, then they would record it on television, but David would attempt the dream viewing during the performance. As usual Jenny would write down what he was seeing and the following day they would watch the recording to check any relevant points. The accuracy was uncanny. David's viewing, it seemed, was as if he was on the actual stage only a couple of metres from the performer.

They told no one about this phenomenon because really, who would believe it? They could hardly believe it themselves and neither of them could come up with any plausible explanation for it. They were using the viewing experiments more for their own enjoyment, as they could see no real purpose behind it all or anything useful to be done with it.

Jenny's mother, Brenda, spent a few days with them over Christmas and, after she had gone home to her little cottage in a Surrey retirement village, David thought he would pick up where he had left off and try another viewing experiment. It was completely unsuccessful.

New Year's Eve was upon them with several live shows on television, one showing Big Ben at Westminster chiming in the new year and he tried over and over again but there was absolutely no sign of the bright light or the eyes returning to him. He did feel some disappointment, as if he could no longer perform some truly clever trick that he had just learned, but he was very glad that they had never told anyone about the viewings, because now he and Jenny would look like a pair of fools.

The new year came and then the months slowly passed with no more dream experiences.

Privately, David and Jenny would discuss with each other the strange events of the past. and one big question that they had both considered to be the most important, was what useful purpose could that ability have ever been put to, anyway? They each came up with a couple of suggestions, which were either silly or impractical. Except one. To assist National Security Services by viewing the top enemies of the state and then inform government what they were doing. They both laughed hilariously when David came up with the idea, but slowly, the more that they thought about it the more it began to make sense. Anyway, it was all in the past now, so none of it mattered anymore. Then on November 23rd it was back again with a bang, and stronger than ever!

There was a feeling of excitement, mixed with a lot of trepidation, that ran through them both. If this thing was going to be used as they had discussed earlier, then from now on their lives were about to change. Would the 'Powers That Be' take David seriously, and would they ever consider using his rather strange ability? Future challenges could be huge and how would they feel if, having started, the ability just fizzled out like a damp firework?

Another question that puzzled them was trying to fathom out the eleven-month gap from last December when it disappeared, to this November when it came back again. Nothing really had changed in their lives, so why was there such a gap in time when there was nothing, and then for this ability to suddenly come back again? In the absence of any better explanation, it was Jenny who put forward an idea.

'I may be way off track here, David, but something has struck me as a bit of a coincidence. Your birthday on December 5th makes you a Sagittarius, doesn't it? The dates for that birth sign are from November 23rd to December 23rd which happens to coincide with old "green eyes" coming and going in your life. What do you think?'

David looked at her for a while before replying. 'I don't honestly follow all that astrology stuff, Jenny, I never have done. I just cannot see the relevance of birth signs and personality traits. I do admit, however, that it's a heck of a coincidence about the dates.'

CHAPTER 2

November 2003

As usual a large sack of mail was delivered to the American Embassy in London on that November morning. As usual security had to check all mail, carefully scanning it before allotting it to its various departments' in-trays. Security had become a major issue since the attack on New York and today was Ruben's day in the 'Secure Box'. Ruben Dexter, known by all as 'Dexie', was a New Yorker himself and had been working there when the twin towers came down.

Taking the bag into the windowless reinforced office he closed the door and got on with the job. He had been attached to the London-based embassy for nearly eleven months now and he loved being here, but both he and his wife Beth sorely missed New York, especially now with Christmas not far away. Eventually he pulled out a letter which looked unusual. It was a long white envelope, post marked Twickenham, stamped a.m. yesterday, with a first-class stamp. The scanner showed it contained just one sheet of paper, not much to worry about. He picked up the phone and called his boss, Bob Crozier.

'Hi Bob, it's Dexie. I'm in the Secure Box and I've got visual on a letter addressed to "The Chief Security Officer" etc. It's handwritten, neat writing. You want me to open it?'

Crozier pondered for a minute.

'Yeah, go ahead, Dexie. It's probably a bill for new locks or something. Stick it in my tray if you think I should see it.' The letter started off normally, with the address and the 'Dear Sir' but soon became questionable.

I am writing to you and not the Ambassador because what I have to say is more a matter for security than it is for politics.

He smiled and mumbled, 'God, you Brits have got a funny way of saying things.' The letter continued:

Please let me assure you that I am not a joker, nor am I mentally unwell and I have no intention of wasting your time or mine. I could never be more serious in my life. The truth is that I am able to give you some particularly important and relevant information regarding a certain person who is desperately wanted for global atrocities, including the unprecedented attacks on New York. If this appears a little vague, then I apologise, but it is only for my own protection, as I am reluctant to put dangerous details on paper. My address and phone number are on this letter. Please arrange a meeting with me and I will give you more information. This is not a hoax and you will not be disappointed. Please treat this as urgent.

Yours truly,
David Sorensen

Dexie read it again, put it back in its envelope and tossed it into the tray marked 'Chief Security.' A mail clerk would soon pick up everything and do the office deliveries.

'That's one for you, Bob. If this guy is a "crazy" then you can sort it out. That's not my job.'

A couple of hours later Dexter's phone rang. It was his boss, Bob Crozier. 'Look, you're free tomorrow, give this guy a call now, arrange a meet for tomorrow and check him out. If you think he's nuts, we'll shelve it. If you sound him out and it grabs you then let me know. You can never tell in this business until you eyeball with someone. Keep me posted, Dexie. Tomorrow I'll be tied up with some meetings, but I'll catch you later.'

Dexie did not feel comfortable with this task, after all it was not really his job to check possible informants. Later that day he called the number and was quickly answered by the author of the letter, David Sorensen. He introduced himself and told the man that he was Embassy Security and that he was checking out what nature of information he had to disclose.

In a well-spoken English accent Sorensen asked, 'Are you the senior security officer?'

'No. That would be my boss, but he is not available right now. I'm the guy you need to talk to. This is my brief and I'll be reporting back, don't worry on that account.'

There was a lengthy pause before the Englishman replied.

'This is going to waste time, I fear, because eventually a report from your senior man will be required to vouch for my sincerity and competence. Would you please tell me his name?'

'No. That sort of information, at least for now, would come under the heading of "classified." For now, sir, I'm all you've got. Do you want to talk to me or not?'

Another lengthy pause, then, 'Very well, but for the sake of my personal safety I will not discuss the nature of information that I can give you. We will need to meet each other, preferably at my house, where I hope to convince you that I am genuine. I am free tomorrow, if that is convenient for you?'

It was now Dexie's turn to pause. If this guy was cracked, then this was going to be a real pain in the butt.

'OK mister. I'll come by car at, let's say 11am. How does that sound?'

'That's fine with me. I look forward to meeting you, Mr. Dexter. Eleven o'clock tomorrow morning then. Goodbye.'

The house was typical of suburbia, a four-bedroom semi with a neat front garden and net curtains hanging at all the windows. Dexie rang the bell and stood back from the door. Sorensen was not what he expected. He was slim, mid-fifties with thinning dark hair and wearing glasses. He could have been a teacher or an accountant. His dark brown eyes had a sad look about them, or maybe he was just plain tired. Handshakes over, he led the American into the lounge and asked him to be seated. The house looked very neat and well decorated, but by American standards, a little too small.

'May I offer you some tea or coffee? I know you chaps are great coffee drinkers.'

'No thanks, I'm good. I would like to get this business done if it's OK with you.'

Sorensen seated himself opposite his visitor and

took a deep breath before starting.

'I will be as direct as I can, Mr. Dexter, but what I have to tell you will sound incredible, but true, nonetheless. In recent times I have become aware that if I concentrate on some person, just prior to going to sleep, then I can see and hear that person in real time, what they are doing and saying at that precise moment. It is as if my sub-consciousness is fully aware of their present predicament, not a dream but an actual awareness of the reality. I cannot change anything or speak to the person, but I can simply view the scene. I am able to speak while in this drowsy state, albeit in a very quiet voice while this process is going on. My wife, Jenny, remains awake and records everything I say on a small recorder. Remember, I cannot alter the scene that I'm viewing. Like a fly on the wall I am simply an observer.'

He stopped when he noticed the look of sheer incredulity on Dexter's face. It was almost comical, his mouth just hung open, so David continued.

'I know how this must sound but let me reassure you that if you were to test me you will find that I am telling the truth.'

'Test you? How can I test you?'

'Well, if you would allow me to take a quick picture of your face on my iPhone, I can concentrate on it just prior to sleep and I could soon be observing you at that very time. Let us kill two birds with one stone. How about you, and maybe your wife, having an evening dinner for example with your boss, the senior security man and his wife? Assuming, of course, that you are both married. Anywhere you like, I don't mind. The following day I can let you know what you were all wearing, what you ate, what you were discussing at the meal and possibly the name and location of the restaurant. That way, your boss will be equally impressed with my ability, sufficiently anyway to send a favourable report to America. I believe that eventually I will have to go to your country to be properly investigated if I am to be of any use.'

Dexter stared at him for a full minute before asking in a slow quiet voice, 'And how the hell do you think you can be of any help to the United States of America?'

'Well, I know it must be imperative to discover the whereabouts of Saddam Hussein and Osama bin Laden. I believe I can visit them in a sleep state and tell you, who is with them and what they are doing, if they are well, ill or wounded. I may even be able to locate their exact whereabouts, I don't know that far ahead, and I won't know until I try. Are you interested in testing me like I said, Mr Dexter?'

Dexter could faintly hear classical violin music playing somewhere in the house and the ticking of a pendulum clock on the wall, when he suddenly realised that the man had stopped talking.

Dexie thought, *What should I say to this guy? How can he be so serious when I know he's talking pure rubbish? I can placate him, I guess. I can string him along. Anything to get out of here. For Crozier's sake I'll set a simple trap which will put this to bed once and for all.*

'OK, Mr. Sorensen, I'll tell you what I'll do. I'll get my boss and his wife to join me and my partner tonight at a little restaurant that we love. Would 8:30 be too early for you to retire? I could make it a little later, but I was just thinking about eating too late, you know?'

'No, that will be fine. I can be asleep by then. I will report on your foursome at dinner between 8:30 and 8:50. I think 20 minutes of personal intrusion into your life is quite enough. Besides, once the vision starts to fade there is no going back. You see, I am actually taken, whilst in a light state of sleep, to these places by these eyes that come to me. I see them at first like a little bar of light, and as they come towards me, I realise that they are in fact a pair of eyes. They get closer and closer until I become attached to them or absorbed by them. From then on, it is they that actually lead me, or my consciousness rather, to where I see things. This state, or condition that I seem to occupy, does not last very long. Whatever energy that causes this phenomenon to occur soon fades and the eyes leave me and eventually disappear as if in a mist. I have no control to bring them back.'

Sorensen remained quiet to study the effect of this revelation, but the American was giving nothing away. If he thought the Englishman was mad, he wasn't showing it. In fact, Dexter was now very annoyed with the whole situation which he felt was plain stupid. Right now he just wanted to get out of this house and return to the sanity of the embassy.

'Very interesting story, Mr. Sorensen. I wish you the best of luck with it. In the meantime, I'll set up the meeting in the restaurant for tonight at 8:30. I'll call you first thing tomorrow to see how it went for you. Oh, one thing I forgot to mention. I'm not married but I do have a partner. His name is Greg.' Sorensen gave a little nod but made no comment.

'We'll speak in the morning then.' He smiled. They shook hands and Dexter left to return to London. Sadly, David felt that the meeting could have gone better.

CHAPTER 3

First Reactions

The American Club in the West End was home from home. It was where you could chill out after work and catch up with friends from the home country or take a meal in the restaurant. There were two pool tables in the bar room which were nearly always busy but tonight Ruben Dexter sat alone waiting for someone. As he sipped his scotch and soda, he checked his watch once again. He was early. He knew Sandy would be along very soon as planned.

Just before 8:30 Sandy strolled in and walked up to Dexter's table with his hand out.

'Hey Buddy, it's good to see you. What's going on? You sounded real strange on the phone!' Dexter shook with laughter.

'Strange? I'll give you strange, OK! You should have been with me this morning Sandy, when I met this English guy who had written into the embassy. Bob Crozier asked me to check him out. This guy reckons he can concentrate on someone just as he is going to sleep and then, as if in a kind of dream, he can see them for real, exactly at that precise time and what they are doing. He actually asked me to set up a test for him tonight, right now in fact. Have you ever heard such crap before?'

'I haven't heard that one before. Where do I come into this?' Sandy queried. The waiter came up and they ordered scotch.

'You, my friend, are my alibi. This weirdo thinks I'm having dinner with Crozier and his wife and my phantom gay partner called Greg.' Sandy burst into laughter.

'Judas Priest, Dexie! If Beth heard you say that, she'd have your balls hanging from the roof top. What made you come up with a yarn like that?'

'Don't you get it? If this guy ever mentions a restaurant or attempts to describe the phantom Greg or the Croziers for that matter, then we will know for sure that he's a lying con man. I need to be with someone I can trust this evening to back up my story to Crozier in case this weirdo keeps pestering us. You don't mind, do you?

'Of course not, you idiot. How long do we have to stay here for, anyway?'

'Pool table has just come free. Let's have a game, just one. I told Beth I wouldn't be too late tonight. That should do it.'

The Following Day

It was Saturday. Both David and Jenny Sorensen had been up very early, had finished breakfast by 8am and were waiting by the telephone for Dexter's call. Since this second episode of dreams had started, they knew it should now be taken seriously and Jenny had bought a handheld voice recorder. She would hold it close to David's mouth when he was in the dream state and made it her job to later transcribe his recordings onto hard copy and keep them in a file. When she first became aware of her husband's new-found ability, she realised how very odd indeed this thing was that had entered their lives. She was instrumental in suggesting that they test him repeatedly to prove to themselves, mainly, that this was a genuine experience they were living through. She knew from the start that her husband was not a fantasist and, weird as it may be, what was happening to him was some kind of 'astral viewing' phenomenon. She didn't understand it any more than he did, but she knew it was genuine. She would softly ask him questions sometimes to clarify a particular situation and being familiar with her voice, he felt safe and could respond. He could easily be distracted from the viewing experience by sudden noise or disturbance and once the hypnotic eyes had gone, he was unable to bring them back at that time. It seemed he only had a small amount of control over the situation and was dependent upon the eyes taking him to the person he had been concentrating on.

Apart from that there was nothing more either of them knew. There was no one they could turn to for advice or guidance, no reference book they could read and if this thing, whatever it was, stayed around for some time then what else could they do except what they were doing now? She asked him once if he felt uncomfortable or stressed when the eyes appeared in front of him and he told her that on the contrary, he felt strangely peaceful and confident when it was happening. However, if he was woken up immediately after the energy had gone then he did feel very tired. It was much better that he should just drop into natural sleep state after the phenomenon was over. It seemed that the experience took a bit of energy from him that required replacing, but he always felt fine after a sleep.

Jenny sat in the lounge and watched David quietly reading her work and occasionally nodding as if in agreement. As they waited for Dexter's call, she let her mind wander a bit. They had no children and, now that Frank was dead, the only living relative was Jenny's mother Brenda. She was very dear to them both and she looked on David like a son she never had, but this latest development would be something that would worry and confuse her if they decided to tell her the whole story. For the time being, at least, they must keep this quiet. If they had children, probably adult by now, it would be different. They might even be of great assistance to them, but that was just wishful thinking. No, this was something that they had to do by themselves, on their own. David had not said as much to her but she knew that he was concerned that people might regard him as a crackpot. She, on the other hand, felt confident in his ability to 'win over' any sceptic that they were bound to encounter along the way. David came across as being a very genuine and truthful person, well spoken, serious and honest and she felt sure that as crazy as the whole thing sounded, he would convince even the worst of the sceptics that his ability was not a trick. She knew that once he had made his mind up on something nothing could shift him and she was equally determined to be his support and ally in any task that lay before him. Maybe it was because there were no children in the marriage, maybe it was that their love for each other was as strong as ever, but

Jenny had always felt very close to David and she knew that if the Americans took this seriously she would be by his side all the way.

'It's a good report, Jen.' David looked up from the sheets of Jenny's transcript.

'Is it particularly helpful, or am I just creating unnecessary paperwork?' she asked.

'Not at all,' he replied. 'I can't remember every detail of what goes on when I'm in with the eyes. I can always remember the main part of the viewing, of course, but looking at every word that I mumbled written out like this brings it all back to me. Besides, although I am not fully aware of it at the time, there are pauses in my speech, sometimes a bit slurred or quiet and seeing it all written out like this is so much clearer, more precise.'

She was happy that her efforts were helpful and, like David, she wondered what to expect if this Dexter chap from the embassy was sufficiently impressed with the report to send it higher up the ladder. She checked her watch and it said nearly eleven o'clock.

'This Dexter chap isn't going to ring, is he? I'd hardly call this 'first thing in the morning, would you?' Jenny looked at her husband and shook her head. 'You've got his number, why not give him a ring now? He doesn't seem to be taking you seriously, does he?'

The embassy switchboard told David that Mr. Dexter was not available until Monday when he would be in at 8am. She looked at her husband's crestfallen face as he told her.

'They are going to waste so much time, Jen. We are already three days into the cycle. If they continue to drag their feet like this the whole month will shoot by and then it's over.'

'You did tell that Dexter chap about the one-month window, didn't you?'

'No. There was no way I could tell him. He was struggling to take in all I had to tell him as it was without me dropping the bombshell that any good I could do for them can only last from November 23rd to December 23rd. Looking at last night's viewing I can see that Dexter thinks I'm a total sham and a time waster. This is going to be a long-haul, Jen.'

They both fell silent for a while, lost in their own thoughts. Jenny spoke first.

'You've never had to convince anyone before about all this, really. This is the first time a total stranger has been exposed to your story and let's face it, David, it is one hell of a story. Don't let this dampen your spirits. Just wait until our Mr Dexter hears what you saw last night. OK, so you will have to wait until Monday to give him the full story but oh boy, when you do give it to him I would love to see the look on his face.'

David smiled and nodded. 'It will be his boss Crozier I will have to convince next. It's not until he reports favourably to someone higher up the ladder that will ultimately control me that we can get this project properly started. Monday morning cannot come fast enough for me. I do feel confident but the stakes are pretty high and this, don't forget, is my first outing. I just feel a wee bit apprehensive, that's all.'

There was no more for them to do. They passed the weekend quietly. On Sunday morning they drove to nearby Richmond Park and enjoyed a long walk together.

CHAPTER 4

Monday Morning Revelation

I t took him three calls but finally David was put through to Ruben Dexter.

'Ah. Mr Sorensen. I was just about to call you,' he lied. 'Very sorry about Saturday. I genuinely forgot it was my weekend off and me and my partner were so busy out of London that I had to leave it to Monday to call you. You just beat me to the phone.'

'Which partner would that be, Mr. Dexter? Would that be Beth or possibly your work partner Sandy? I only ask because we both know, don't we, that your gay partner Greg is a figment of your imagination. By the way, it's true I think, that the "classified" Bob Crozier didn't know a thing about any "meal for four" on Friday evening, did he? Good job Sandy was available to give you an alibi in case this weirdo Brit pushes his luck. What do you reckon, Mr Dexter?' David had spoken slowly and confidently.

There was a long embarrassing silence before Dexter eventually replied and when he did his voice was low and deliberate. 'Mr. Sorensen, you have my full and undivided attention as of this moment. As they say, the ball is now in your court and I am listening to whatever you have to suggest. Please go ahead.'

'It's what I said at the beginning, sir. I need to speak to Mr. Crozier because you know that nothing will move without his say so. I have a written report for you which describes what you were wearing on Friday evening and how you got to the American Club a bit early and had a glass of scotch while you waited for Sandy. It describes what Sandy was wearing and how you both had another scotch before having one game of pool. You won, by the way, but it was close. He wanted another game, if you remember, but you had promised Beth that you would be home at a reasonable time. Does this sound familiar at all? The written report is more thorough than this sketchy outline, of course.'

Dexter spoke contritely. 'That does not sound sketchy to me. That sounds too Goddamn close for comfort. I'm sorry I tried to jerk you around, man, but you saw through it all, didn't you? I don't know how you did it, but you've impressed the hell out of me and that's for sure. Let me speak to, er, well you already know his name is Crozier and I guess the next person to speak to you will be him. Is that OK with you?'

The two men agreed that David's report should be

sent to Dexter by e-mail, who would present it personally on hard copy to Crozier with his own comments and opinions. Crozier was fully briefed by lunchtime that same day. He appeared very calm and asked Dexter for the Englishman's phone number.

'Hello, Mr. Sorensen. You already know my name, I believe; this is Bob Crozier. I have read your report and I find it very interesting indeed. However, before I can put my name to any recommendation I will need to do a little research of my own. You do understand, don't you?'

David was delighted that at last things were moving in the right direction.

'Yes, of course, but I do have to meet you at some stage because I don't know what you look like and that is a necessary requirement if you wish to be involved personally in researching me. I'm sure that is what you have in mind.'

'Yes, absolutely. I want no one else involved. Can I send a car to pick you up from home in say two hours? I cannot leave the office today and I guess we have to meet somewhere, don't we, so it might as well be at the embassy. The driver will be briefed to get you to my office. The meeting should not be too long and of course we will give you a ride home when it's finished. Will that be OK?'

Sorensen agreed and went upstairs to change into something more appropriate than his gardening clothes. First impressions count a lot. Jenny was shopping at the supermarket so he rang her mobile and gave her the news. She was as keen as her husband to get involved.

'Should I come along with you, David?' she asked. 'Will he want to see me also? I mean I did write out the report, and he may want to question me, do you think?'

'No, my dear. It won't be necessary. This meeting is all about me getting to see his face so I will have something to focus on tonight. He will certainly have something devious up his sleeve to test me, which of course should not be a problem. I'll be home soon enough, darling, and I will probably need your help tonight. Bye for now.'

The pick-up was prompt and the driver got him to the embassy in quick time. It was a typical gloomy winter afternoon, the streetlights were just coming on and a light drizzle of rain had started as they entered the building. The driver helped him through security and a visitor's pass was issued to David who was then taken to Crozier's office.

Both men were a little surprised by each other's countenance. As David entered the room he saw a short, dark-haired man with a thick rounded moustache, almost comical. Crozier was powerfully built and as they shook hands the Englishman felt the strength of his grip.

Not quite what he expected from the soft voice he heard over the telephone. On the other hand, Sorensen was lean and tall, in his mid-fifties with dark penetrating eyes. His neatly cut hair was slightly thinning at the front and he was dressed in light-coloured chinos, tweed jacket and cream roll-neck sweater. Once they were seated on either side of the large desk Crozier stared hard at David. 'Is what you do some type of clever trick? I have to ask that first, before you begin to get out of your depth. You see, if this becomes a waste of time for all of us it would be most unfortunate, do you understand?'

David looked across the desk and could see a very serious, almost aggressive face looking back. The veiled threat was not entirely lost upon him. 'Let me assure you right from the start that what I achieve is not a trick,' he replied in a slow and cultured voice. 'It is not magic, nor is it my imagination. I cannot fully explain how or why it happens but it does. It is a phenomenon, that's the only way I can describe it. Test me any way you wish. I am not bothered.'

'Oh yes. I intend to, Mr. Sorensen. This very

evening, in fact. Give me a time that is suitable for your "requirement," for want of a better word, and I will call you just prior to that time and tell you what I have in mind.'

'Ten thirty would be fine for me. I find that this all happens when I'm in a drowsy state just before proper sleep and it doesn't last for too long. Sometimes only for a few minutes. It's very strange.'

'Yeah. Whatever. I'll call you at around 10:15 tonight to explain how I wish to test you. Have you any questions and have you seen enough of me to keep in your memory?'

'That's "no" to the first and "yes" to the second, thank you.'

Crozier stood up, thrust out his hand and said, 'Until 10:15 tonight then.'

As David shook hands he thought, *Mm. That was quick. Not even the offer of coffee.* He had the feeling he was being dismissed. He smiled, nodded and turned to leave the room. Just as he reached the door Crozier spoke out.

'Tell me something, Sorensen. This is all about the money, isn't it? Of course it is! That's a possible twenty-five million dollars for OBL and a further twenty-five million for Saddam. Come on, just be honest, will ya?'

David stared hard and long before answering. 'You sound a little cynical, Mr. Crozier. May I remind you of two things? Firstly, it was not me who set the bounty for these two fugitives from justice. Nor was it me who created the priority for their capture. I would say the rewards simply reflect the urgency, or desperation rather, that not only your country but the whole western world feels at this time. There appears to be a determination to overthrow western civilisation through acts of destruction and terror, epitomised by 9/11. Al Qaeda is hell bent on global jihad against the infidels and Saddam is a murdering dictator waging war on his neighbours as well as killing his own people and bringing instability to the whole region. In addition, how can your president ever consider the Iraq war a success while Saddam is in hiding and remains a threat to the future? If I can help to locate these two evil monsters then I would say your cynicism is ill placed, to say the least.'

Crozier gave a wry smile and put his hands up in a gesture of surrender.

'We will speak later. I'll call you from my house.'

Through the wet glistening streets of London and out into suburbia he looked out of the car windows, but in his mind, he kept the image of Crozier's thickset features. He wanted it to go well tonight. He considered calling Jenny on his mobile to give her the news of the meeting but he thought the driver might report back details of the conversation. There was nothing to hide, of course, but he felt they could talk more easily at home.

CHAPTER 5

Put to the Test

D avid was already prepared for bed when the phone rang spot on time. It was Bob Crozier.

'I've left this call to the last minute so I will know that you could not possibly prepare anything beforehand. It's a security check of my own, if you like. Now listen carefully. This is the test. At 10:30 I will go into my garage where my car is parked. I want you to simply note the colour, the make, the model and the registration number of that car. I will also shine a flashlight onto the dash and I want you to record the exact mileage. You got all that? You can call me in the office tomorrow morning, sooner the better after 8:30am OK?'

David agreed and the phone cut off. He got into bed and his wife lay next to him, the recorder at the ready by the side of his pillow. He clearly recalled the strong, heavy features of the American and kept the image firmly in his mind. His breathing became slower and deeper and very soon he drifted into a drowsy state of relaxation, not unconscious but more like floating in the moonlight. In the distance he saw the bright strip of light coming towards him. He wasn't worried, he knew by now what it was and what the procedure was going to be. The strip of light approached him at speed but stopped a short distance from his face. As usual he could now make out the eyes. They were bright, unblinking and stared directly into his own. Slowly they moved towards him, closer and closer until they were blurred then suddenly, *pop!* He was somewhere else and it was he who was now looking through those very eyes at a place that was totally new to him.

Bob Crozier was lying on a comfortable-looking sofa in a large sitting room. He held a glass of something milky in his hand and waited for the half-hour to come.

David noticed that the man was wearing a deep red tracksuit with grey-coloured bands around the cuffs, neck and hem but that probably wasn't important. Crozier had been specific about what he wanted.

As if on cue he jumped off the sofa and made his way to a door in the kitchen, beyond which was the integral garage. David immediately saw the car, which was a Mercedes SUV. Playing by the rules, Crozier went to the rear of the car and shone a light onto the boot lid. It was the ML 320 model but oddly the front and rear number plates had been covered with silver gaffer tape. He next opened the driver's door, put on the ignition and the dashboard lit up brightly and the mileage was clearly shown as 11,166. He didn't waste any time and soon the car was locked once more, the lights turned off and he returned to the kitchen where he drained that milky glass before turning in for bed himself.

As he was about to switch off the kitchen lights a tan-coloured Persian cat appeared and brushed up against the man's legs. He looked down at it affectionately. 'Come on then, Cleo,' he said. 'Last drink before bed and that's it. You got that?'

He bent down and tickled the cat's ears before taking a carton out of a large double-door fridge and pouring some milk into a glass bowl. He left the cat to drink in the darkness and made his way upstairs. Upon entering the bedroom David noticed a woman, most probably the man's wife, sitting up in bed and reading. He had seen enough for now and struggled to wake up. As he opened his eyes, he saw Jenny and smiled. When he closed them again the guiding eyes had gone. The whole scene only took five or six minutes and forcing himself awake, was his way of keeping some control on the viewing.

Next Morning

Crozier hardly had time to drink his black coffee when his phone rang. He listened quietly and intently as David read out the events of last night's viewing from Jenny's manuscript. He decided not to leave out any details. He told him everything about the car and also described the red track suit, the cat called Cleo and the drink of milk. As he came to the end of his report he asked, 'Just one thing puzzles me, Mr. Crozier. Your number plates, front and rear. They were taped over. What was that about? I'm afraid the guiding eyes are not X-ray. I couldn't see the car number. Sorry about that.'

Crozier chuckled from deep down in his stomach. 'Damn you, Sorensen, but you were good, you delivered exactly like you said. Apart from the fact that I don't like too many people knowing my car number, I taped up those plates within two minutes of putting down the phone to you last night. It was the last thing I did before you went off into your drowsy state. Nobody on this planet could have known that, there was no way. I did it as an extra test.'

'The question is, are you convinced now? Have I passed the test?'

'I don't pretend to understand what's going on with you, but I feel confident enough to put my signature on a report to Washington DC explaining what I've witnessed. From then on it's up to the FBI whether they bother with you immediately or let you stew on a back burner. My part in this story will be over, except to liaise between you and them if they want you over there.'

David hesitated before replying. He knew this next bit would have to come out at some time, but he was not looking forward to the expected reaction.

'That brings me to a difficult position, Mr. Crozier. You see speed is very important right now as I only have up until December 23rd before this ability disappears. In other words, this occurs once a year between November 22nd and December 23rd, so it seems so far. After that date I would have to wait eleven months to reconnect again. I really do not know why this is, but that's the way it seems to be working. That's why speed is everything if we are to make any headway. I cannot be on anyone's "back burner."'

Crozier looked down at his desk and took several deep breaths.

'This story gets crazier by the minute! What, in God's name, have those dates got to do with any damn thing?'

David looked sheepish. 'Well, it may possibly be that as I was born on December 5th. That makes me Sagittarius. Those dates are the dates of my birth sign, namely Sagittarius. I know this presents a big problem but it's out of my control. I am genuinely sorry. If I could change the way things are, do you think I wouldn't?'

'Judas H. Priest, Sorensen! This is bullshit! Just as I was getting the feel for this gig you come up with this ball breaker. Who the hell is going to take you seriously, man?'

'I know! I bloody well know!' David shouted back. 'But think positively, will you? Look at this as just one job, OK? We do have time to complete one job, plenty of time if you can treat this project as urgent. This is too important to throw out.'

'Why didn't you come forward months ago and tell us about this ability, or whatever you call it?'

'How could I?' David retorted. 'How seriously would you have taken me then? I couldn't have been tested months ago and it's only the testing that makes me a viable project.'

'I will put it all in my report just like you have said. It won't be me that decides whether this can fly or not. I promise that I will expedite my report and I will contact you the minute I hear anything. Sorensen?

Don't hold your breath, son.' He clicked off the phone and immediately dialled Ruben Dexter's extension.

'Dexie. Do a full security check on this guy Sorensen ASAP.'

'Shall I go through Five or Special Branch?'

'Keep Five out of this. If this guy is any use to us at all, and Five knows about him, we lose control. Use The Branch and just tell them it's an urgent emigration enquiry. I want everything on Sorensen, his complete background, religion, politics, education, marriages, employments, kids, associates etc. You know the score. Let me know the minute you have completed, and Dexie? Treat this as urgent, will ya? From now on this becomes classified. No loose chat, no mention of the guy again to anyone. If Sandy ever brings it up in conversation just tell him it was all BS, like you thought it would be.'

'I've got that, Chief, no problem. Just between us though, is this man for real? I mean, is he going to be the big breakthrough?'

Crozier thought for some moments before replying wearily, 'I wish I knew the answer to that one, Dexie, I really do. Once Washington gets my report then it's out of our hands. The Bureau can sweat over the guy.'

CHAPTER 6

Meeting 'The Man'

They took the flight from London Heathrow to Ronald Reagan National Airport near Washington DC and landed mid-morning. Two Federal Agents met up with them when they had cleared immigration and helped them with their luggage. Agent Linda Leoni was petite and friendly, but the guy who did the driving, Agent Sam McGill, was very quiet and hardly looked at them.

'We'll take you both to your hotel first, give you a little time to settle in but then it's to Hoover for you Mr. Sorensen, pronto. Someone there is waiting to meet you and it seems that it's important. If you don't mind doing the unpacking, Mrs. Sorensen, while your husband is busy, that will save some time,' said the female agent and Jenny nodded.

'Hoover?' David questioned.

'Yeah,' she replied. 'The J. Edgar Hoover building, to be precise. Headquarters, FBI.'

'Who will I be seeing there?' he asked.

'You'll soon find out everything you need to know,

don't worry. Your hotel is good. Not Vegas, mind you, but small and comfortable and the breakfasts are excellent. You eat out for lunch and dinner at your own expense, but the hotel bill is taken care of, even room service, so make the most of it. OK?'

The drive took about thirty minutes from the hotel to the Hoover Building in Pennsylvania Avenue and David sat quietly in the back of the car and admired the city.

Eventually they arrived at a large, impressive building. The man stayed with the vehicle and the female agent took David into reception and helped him to clear security. He was finally given a visitor's pass which he wore on his lapel and the female agent made a phone call to someone called Mr. Casey announcing their arrival in the building. They next made their way to one of several lifts on the main reception floor. They got out on the fifth floor and Agent Leoni approached a door with the words 'J.D. Casey. Ops. Intel' written in gold colour on a dark wooden background. She knocked on the door and they were invited in.

The solitary occupant was a tall, heavily built man in his early to mid-fifties, David guessed. He was dressed in dark blue trousers with pale blue open-neck shirt.

'Thanks, Linda. I'll call you soon to take him back to the hotel. Keep the car on standby. This won't take too long. Take a seat, Mr. Sorensen. Coffee?' He didn't wait for an answer but walked over to a table which housed a coffee jug on an electric ring.

'Yes please. I like it white with two sugars, if that's OK,' David answered as he looked around the office. The man had his back to him and gave a sardonic smile.

White with sugar! God, that's no way to drink coffee, he thought to himself. He made two large cups of the stuff and put the white one down in front of David. As he sipped from his cup his piercing eyes studied the Englishman without speaking. His mouth was thin and downturned, almost cruel, and his neatly combed hair was thinning a little on the top.

Suddenly, he put down his cup and thrust out his right hand.

'Welcome to Washington. I'm J.D. Casey and I run Operational Intelligence, like it says on the door. The only person in this building that you and your wife will have any contact with is me. Is that clear? You speak to no one as to why you are here, and you answer nobody's questions, except mine of course. I've read the reports from London and that is why you are here. You must stay at the Hotel Caribou, where you were taken, and you must agree to follow my instructions to the letter. Only that way can I guarantee your safety. The hotel is paid for by us and, as a couple, you and your wife will receive jointly $150 a day for each day that you work for us with an advance of $150 which will cover today. Any questions, so far?' Casey spoke quickly with a 'no nonsense' tone in his voice. He was a man used to giving orders and expected them to be carried out.

David smiled as he identified the controlling element in the man's persona. 'No questions so far, thank you. I am looking forward to working with you,' he replied.

'I've taken note of your time-scale restriction, your short "window of opportunity," so to speak, and I don't pretend to understand how or why that should be relevant. However, if you can deliver the goods like Dexter and Crozier seem to think, then we are in business. But if you screw up, Mr. Sorensen…' He paused for maximum effect. 'Well, you and your wife will be on the very next plane back to London. Is that crystal? Good! Now then, you're probably tired from your flight, so I'm going to let you go. Tonight, at 2200, I will be home and I will set you a little test of my own, to put my own mind at ease. A car will pick you up at 0900 and bring you here for your report.

Your wife will not be needed tomorrow so I guess she can do some retail therapy, should she choose to. You will both be given cell phones to keep in touch, but let me remind you just this once, neither of you discuss anything to do with this assignment or the Bureau over the telephone. Your calls will be monitored, so we will know. Don't forget, 2200 hours tonight and I'll see you in the morning. Nice meeting you.'

'Are you asking me to think of you tonight at ten o'clock so I can report on your actions at home, etc?' David asked.

'Sure. Is that a problem? Have you seen enough of me to remember what I look like?'

'Well, not really, sir. I've only just met you and I do need to have a fairly good recollection of a face before this begins to work properly.'

The American picked up his phone and clicked an extension number. 'Linda? He's ready to return to the Caribou. Pick up a couple of cell phones booked out to the Sorensens and $150 cash also in their names. Oh, and Linda? One last thing. Get a facial of me from records, will ya? It doesn't have to be big and give it to the guy, OK?' He looked at David and nodded.

'She'll pick you up at reception. She's good, she'll help you. See you in the morning.'

With that he commenced reading some paperwork.

David had been dismissed, so he quietly rose from his chair and headed for the door. 'Thank you for the coffee,' he said.

Casey never looked up or spoke, he just raised his hand as 'goodbye.'

By the time he got back to the Hotel Caribou it was afternoon and he and Jenny were hungry. The sky was dull and it was cold outside so they took a short walk to the nearest diner where they could eat and discuss what had happened at Hoover House. As David was recalling the events, he copied Casey's staccato delivery and New York accent which made Jenny laugh and splutter her coffee. They both agreed that this was a heck of an adventure and were looking forward to doing some real work with the Bureau.

Before the evening was through, they were both very tired and were glad as ten o'clock approached. Having had a hot shower, David was first in bed and studied the small passport photo of J.D. Casey. He was thinking over how the conversation had gone in the FBI office when suddenly he felt his eyes glazing over and he entered a state of complete relaxation. He was drifting pleasantly across an evening sky when there, in the distance, he saw it. It was like a strip of glowing magnesium and it came towards him at speed, stopping suddenly without slowing down in front of his face. He stared into those unblinking, hypnotic green eyes as they got closer and larger until he appeared to simply go inside them.

With a smile he realised that he was in Casey's study and, being a bit early, had caught him off guard. He was sitting back in a large swivel chair with his stockinged feet up on the desk and was reading the sports page of a newspaper. There was an empty Budweiser bottle on his desk and he held a smart pewter and glass tankard in his right hand. Through the eyes, David had time to acquaint himself with the room which was decorated rather expensively in old colonial style with beautiful dark wood furniture and a large stone fireplace. The lighting came from discreetly placed free-standing lamps, but the main feature was a glorious, crackling log fire that threw its warmth and some light into the room. Above the fireplace, attached to the wall, were a pair of gleaming crossed cavalry swords, and around the room were fitted bookshelves with a great variety of books filling them. There was also an attractive drinks cabinet made mostly from dark wood with a glass front. A soft light from within lit up two glass shelves containing bottles of spirit and drinking glasses.

David heard a high-pitched peeping sound and saw Casey look at his watch and switch off the alarm.

He drained his tankard, tossed the newspaper onto the desk and brought his feet to the floor. He picked up a large note pad and a felt-tipped pen and made his way over to a leather armchair by the fireside. He sat down in it and after a few seconds of thought he took the felt marker and scrawled the word 'Jacksonville' across the top sheet of the pad.

'Are you watching?' he muttered softly. 'You've got five seconds, that's all.'

He then quickly ripped off the top sheet from the pad, screwed it up and threw it onto the burning logs. He next wrote 'Dallas' on the next sheet, waited five seconds and threw that also, onto the fire. 'Chicago' came next and that too joined the others in the flames.

'That was easy, now try this. I'll give you ten seconds for this one,' Casey muttered and in smaller letters he wrote, 'Abu Ubaida MASRI, the holy warrior. AKA Muddabir PASHTO.'

Ten seconds later it went into the fire and he checked his watch. It showed 10:07 and 50 seconds. He wrote that down quickly and that soon joined the others in the flames. All of this, David could see quite clearly and as he reported everything in a soft voice, so Jenny recorded it on their little voice recorder.

Casey seemed to ponder for a short while then, leaving his chair, he went over to a light switch by the door. He kept the pad and marker in one hand and flicked off the switch with the other. The room went into near darkness, with just the ambient light from the fire sending out a soft glow. He walked over to a narrow cupboard and opening the door he leaned inside and placed the pad onto an empty shelf. It was really dark in this place and Casey could not really see what he was about to write, but the vision from the guiding eyes seemed to splash out a ray of soft, fluorescent green light and David saw the words 'Angela Tamasi' hurriedly written down and burned.

Only ten minutes had passed since he had started his test, but Casey seemed satisfied with what he had done. He returned to his desk and continued reading his newspaper. David felt that it was all over for now so, as he had learned to do in the past, he forced himself out of this drowsy, half-sleep state by opening his eyes and looking around momentarily. When he closed them again the eyes had gone and he drifted off into a deeper sleep.

At nine the next morning he was picked up by car and, with the recorder in his pocket, he was driven to the Hoover Building for his first serious meeting with the man who could make things happen. As he sat in Casey's office, he produced the voice recorder and briefly explained how he had inadvertently started a little early and that he had seen Casey reading the sports page. He then switched on the recorder and watched Casey's face intently as the voice reported so accurately everything the FBI man had done in his study the previous night. The man never moved a muscle but stared hard, downwards at his desk until he heard the words 'Angela Tamasi' spoken. He stood up quickly and gasped, 'How the fuck did you see that?'

David watched him carefully as he stood looking out of the office window and then asked, 'What was Jacksonville, Dallas and Chicago all about? Is there any connection with anything?'

Casey turned and studied him for some seconds before answering. 'Oh hell, that was the easy bit. Just my initials, that's all, J.D.C., but tell me about the last name. Nobody round here knows that name. It's on my file, of course, but you could never have known that. How did you get that name, mister? I wrote it in near total darkness and even then, it stayed for only three seconds before the fire got it!'

Calmly and patiently David explained, 'It seems that even in the darkness the eyes can see clearly. Your writing pad was bathed in a soft green light that made the words very clear, but I'm surprised that you could see what you were writing in that darkened cupboard. May I ask who the lady is?'

The FBI man went back to staring out of the window but eventually he replied, 'I was adopted as an infant by the Casey family. When I left college, I wanted to trace my birth mother but discovered that she had died two years earlier. Her name was Angela Tamasi.' He seemed deep in thought, or lost in memories for a while, but when he spoke again it was business as usual.

'I'll need that recorder of yours to download the report. I'll erase the chip when I'm done and you can have the machine back. Pack your things up, you and your wife will be moving to a new location tomorrow. Somewhere private and safer than the hotel. You speak to no one about why you're here. Is that clear? Not even to the agents who pick you up each day. This is for your safety and for Jenny's also. As from this moment you will be working on an FBI project which must be regarded with utmost security. It will have a code name of Operation Eagle Eye. Is all this crystal clear to you? Have you any questions?' David shook his head. 'OK. Chill out for the rest of this day. Tomorrow you move to your new place. You will be picked up at ten hundred by an agent and taken there. The agent will stay with you to show you around. Both you and your wife will be brought here for sixteen hundred. There will be a briefing first, photographs you can study and maybe some important questions you may be able to answer, in time. There is some serious work to be done here, Sorensen, and tomorrow we start.'

David felt his heart rate increase as a surge of adrenaline was released into his body. At last this journey was about to begin and he felt the excitement of being involved in something so important. Everything that had gone before this day was all just a preparation and now he could move forward. People would take him seriously at last. This was going to be a big challenge and he could hardly wait to tell Jenny how the afternoon had gone.

CHAPTER 7

Settling In

The next day they moved into a smart and very secure house in suburbia. Obviously an FBI safe house, it was fitted with CCTV cameras front and rear, secure locks on every door and panic alarms in every room. From outside it looked like every other house in the street, complete with a decking area at the rear with large BBQ, a double integral garage and good garden lighting. This was going to be their home for as long as they found David useful. Although the front porch door was painted white like all the others, this one was made of steel with two locks, one electric and one with an unusual security key. The garage door had a steel grille behind it which operated electronically. The adjoining door from the garage into the house was similarly secure.

It was Jenny's first time in America and her entrance and security clearance into the FBI Headquarters was an awesome experience for her. She was both nervous and excited to be meeting this man Casey, about whom David had told her. She was expecting him to be a serious, abrupt, tough guy with a no-nonsense attitude. Instead he turned out to be respectful and caring towards her, which surprised David, considering his rather business-like attitude displayed at their first meeting.

They had brought with them an overnight bag each, as was requested, but no explanation had been given and the Sorensens knew better than to query it. Casey's desk was now covered in photographs. Some were of Saddam Hussein but others were of various Arab men in robes or uniform that the English couple did not recognise. There were also some aerial photographs of some camp-type locations and two or three limousines with their number plates highlighted. The couple were invited to spend time studying these pictures, all of which were stamped with 'Top Secret' in red at the upper right corner. Jenny was pleased to be considered a team player by this man. Being taken into his confidence meant a lot to her as she wanted more than anything to be a support to her husband.

As they pored over the images, J.D. had been on the telephone. When he finished speaking he replaced the handset and turned to the couple at his desk.

'You may have guessed already that your main objective is locating Saddam Hussein. That priority comes straight from the White House, OK? We know where OBL is, he's hiding in the Tora Bora mountains which he knows so well. Apart from bombing the hell out of the place, we've got American and British special forces combing the whole area. It won't take long before he's history. There's no closure with the Iraq war while Saddam is on the loose. He's our target now, our number one priority.'

David wanted to explain the process of how this could work to J.D. and to let him know that this project was not going to be without its difficulties. For a start he had never tried to find a location in an area that was totally foreign to him, and he wasn't sure how he was going to face that challenge.

'Mr. Casey, I must mention a couple of things to clarify my position. You know, until I am in with the eyes I cannot predict what is going to happen exactly. Not a clue, really. Through Jenny you can ask me some simple questions and I will do my best to comply. Any loud noises or distracting voices will awaken me fully and that will be it, for that night at least. In the past Jenny has been able to speak to me gently in my half-sleep state and, because I am comfortable with her voice, I can react to the request and the eyes will take me there. For me this is definitely an experiment, sir. I hope to adapt along the way. Incidentally, may I ask where this is going to happen? We have our overnight bags so I presume we are not going back to our house tonight. Am I right?'

'Correct. We have a special suite right here. It's a surveillance suite, actually. Sensitive microphones, comfortable and practical. You will not be disturbed but everything you say will be recorded. It's better that way, more professional and the recordings will all be stored in numerical order. Jenny can wear an earpiece and questions I may have I can put to her and she can then pass them on to you. I will hear every word through my headphones from another room. You won't be needing your little voice recorder from now on. By the way, both of you, feel free to call me JD.'

After the meeting David stayed behind to familiarise himself with the photographs, while Casey took Jenny to the suite that she and David would occupy that night. It wasn't luxurious but it was clean, practical and well laid out. There was a small wardrobe, a double bed and a dressing table with a large mirror attached to the wall above it. There was also an en-suite bathroom. He watched as she tested the bed and pillows for comfort. Her beauty and self-assurance were not lost on him and he found himself looking at her more than was necessary.

Maybe David was going to be the star, hopefully so anyway, but his wife was certainly the inspiration

71

behind him. He was a lucky guy.

'If we don't need our voice recorder then where is the microphone in here?' she asked.

'Check out the top of the headboard. You'll see two chrome grilles, one left and one right. Microphones are in there. They are very sensitive and pick up every whisper, every sigh.'

'How is this going to work tonight with the time lag between the States and Iraq? Will it be OK if David makes a viewing in their daytime, wherever that may be?'

'Sure it is,' he smiled. 'In fact, if he does make contact, we don't want a viewing of Saddam asleep, do we? Washington is about eight and a half hours behind Kabul by my last reckoning, so night-time Sunday here will be early morning prayer time over there. The big test, as I see it, is in trying to identify the exact location of the target. We are absolutely sure that Saddam is still in Iraq but is being hidden by his supporters.'

Jenny had finished putting away their few overnight possessions and as she went to leave the room she was aware that JD was standing in the doorway. She felt a little uncomfortable as her intention to leave was quite obvious. He looked down into her eyes before speaking. 'I never asked you what your husband did for a living. How is it that he can just leave home for the USA without concerns about his job?' In fact, JD knew everything about them both but his question was simply to make conversation.

'He was a graphic designer for a company that was big enough to have its own graphics department. David was head of department when the company hit a bad patch and decided to ditch their own GD and put their requirements out to freelance people. David and all the others were made redundant. It was then that he discovered this unusual ability. He hasn't worked for over a year. If this works out, I guess he won't need to work again. Did you not know any of this before now? I would have expected you people to have given us a thorough background check before we left Britain,' she stated.

JD smiled and nodded. 'Sure we did. I just like to hear you talking. Shall we say bedtime tonight will be at midnight? I know it's on the late side but if contact is made, I would prefer to hear of some activity if at all possible. I will let your two agents know about pick-up time etc. We can meet up again here at twenty-three thirty. OK?'

Slowly he stood back from the doorway and let Jenny pass.

'Yes, of course. I will let David know,' she replied and went back to JD's office to join her husband.

CHAPTER 8

Serious Discovery

Although David and Jenny didn't know it, the large wall mirror above the dressing table was, in fact, two way. In the next room Casey was seated behind the mirror and prepared himself to witness a very unusual event. In front of him was a small control panel on a shelf which allowed him to record proceedings and to communicate with Jenny via her earpiece. David was dressed for bed but she was still in her day clothes and pulled the easy chair close to him. He had seen enough of Saddam's face that afternoon, so he settled into the bed and relaxed. His breathing was slow and rhythmical and he lay perfectly still. The bedroom was dimly lit with subtle uplighters and from his darkened room next door Casey could see the bed clearly through the glass. He pulled on a pair of headphones over his ears and adjusted a small microphone that protruded from the control panel. By pushing down on a button on the panel he could speak to Jenny. The scene was now set.

After only a couple of minutes David jumped involuntarily and appeared to be distressed. 'I am falling! Falling through darkness very quickly. I can't see anything but I just have the feeling of falling. This is very odd. I do not like this.'

'I'm here, David. You are safe. Everything is alright. Just breathe deeply and stay calm.'

He was moving his head from side to side and breathing quickly.

'Is it always like this?' JD asked quietly into Jenny's earpiece.

'No. Never been distressed before. I'll see how this is playing out and if I think he is in some real difficulty I will wake him up immediately,' she replied.

David calmed down and spoke quietly. 'I can see the bar now. It's in the distance and it's coming towards me but not as fast as it has before. I don't know why.'

He remained calm as the eyes approached him and very slowly, he became one with them.

'I am in a small yard near to a rundown building. Shabby, flat roof, single-storey building. Looks dilapidated. Quite small.' He remained silent for a couple of minutes and then continued. 'I see no movement here, so I am going inside.'

Less than a minute passed.

'Good God, it's him. He is here. He is seated at a little wooden table and eating from a tin dish. This is definitely Saddam Hussein, but you would hardly recognise him. He has become dishevelled and he looks older with long white beard and hair.'

JD flicked the switch forward and spoke softly to Jenny through the earpiece. 'Ask him how he can be so sure it is Saddam. Could this man be a double?'

As she repeated the question, almost in a whisper, David shook his head slowly.

'No. Not a double. It's him alright. The eyes wouldn't take me to an imposter when I had been concentrating on someone else. No, it's definitely him.'

Jenny next asked a question of her own.

'Is there some way you can find a location of where this place is?' she asked.

'I will go out and have a look around. By the way, he is armed. He is wearing a gun in a holster and there is an automatic weapon of some kind, looks like an AK-47, leaning up against the wall.'

A few tense minutes passed then David mumbled that there was water nearby, a river really, and then open countryside. He thought everything looked deserted. 'There is some old-fashioned farming stuff around… very old and rusty. I can also see some… No, no! The light is fading. The vision is going, it's going.' He trailed off and taking a deep breath, he turned onto his side and went quiet. He appeared to be asleep.

'Jenny, get him back will ya? We haven't got anywhere yet. We haven't done anything.' JD spoke urgently into his microphone.

'No use,' she replied. 'The eyes have gone. It's out of his control now. He is in ordinary sleep state and will stay like that for the rest of the night. Tomorrow is another day, JD. That's about it for now. Goodnight.'

She took out her earpiece, placed it in the bedside drawer and started to undress. She had no idea that she was being watched right until she also fell asleep by David's side. JD removed his headphones and hung them up on the wall hook.

'Damn! So disappointing,' he muttered to himself. 'We've hardly moved an inch. Still, at least we have made contact.'

They were up early next morning, and quickly washed, dressed and left the Hoover Building before JD had even arrived in the office. They took a cab to the nearest diner and sat down to a decent breakfast. As they ate, they talked about last night's vision and David agreed with Jenny that he should try to control the eyes to find more clues as to Saddam's location. He had never actually tried to control the eyes before and simply relied upon them to go wherever they wanted to take him. They had almost finished when David's mobile rang. It was JD. 'Goddamn you! Where the hell are you and how dare you just leave the building without asking first or checking out?' he shouted. 'Have you no idea of the security risk you present? Any half-baked Jihadist would waste you both in a heartbeat if he knew what you were trying to do. Do you think this is a game we are playing? I need to cover your asses 24/7 from now on. Where exactly are you?'

David could feel the anger down the phone.

'I apologise for my thoughtlessness. Clearly, I wasn't thinking but, in my defence may I just say that this is all very new to us and we are not familiar with such security. We were so hungry we thought we would grab a quick breakfast before returning to our house for a shower and some fresh clothing. Are we to be cooped up like prisoners or do we get some free time to look around this beautiful city?'

His question was ignored but JD snapped back, 'Are you going to tell me where you are or do I have to track you through your mobile?' David gave the name and location of the diner and the phone went dead.

Within a few minutes Agents Leoni and McGill sauntered into the diner and beckoned the pair to follow them.

'Hey. What did you do to piss off Casey like that? I've never seen him so mad,' Leoni asked with a broad smile. 'Who are you people, anyway? Are you involved in one of Casey's projects? They sat quietly in the back of the car. They had been thoroughly admonished and were feeling sore from the experience. This questioning could be a test to see if they could keep their mouths shut.

It was Jenny who eventually replied, 'We have been instructed to speak to no one about our presence here. As FBI agents I am sure you both understand that.'

The two agents glanced casually at each other and nothing more was said as they headed towards the suburban safe house. Just as they arrived agent Leoni turned to Jenny. 'Take my card. It has my number on it. If you guys need any help, any information or advice or even just a bit of sightseeing, you call me, OK? We won't crowd you or make our tail obvious but we will be there for you. It's our assignment, no problem.'

'Thank you,' Jenny smiled. 'Can I say something? We wish to cooperate fully at all times. We would not be here in your country as your guests, if that was not the case.'

Leoni nodded sympathetically. 'We know you're not the bad guys and we know that your security, your safety, is paramount. We know that much about you, but that's all. And hey, that's cool. We don't need to know any more than that.'

'How will this actually work between us?' David asked. 'I mean, if we wanted to go somewhere, other than the Hoover Building, shopping, sightseeing, anything, are we to tell you first and then just go, or do you have to accompany us all the time?'

It was McGill who replied and they were surprised to hear his deep southern drawl. 'We pick you up and take you home when you are working with JD. Any down time that you have you take a cab but not until we can tail you. You always check with us first and wait until we give you the green light. When you're on foot, in a shopping mall, or whatever, one of us will be following you. We are not your full-time taxi service but we will always be looking out for you. For the time being, anyway.'

Once inside the house they locked themselves in securely. Jenny got into the shower while David tried to phone JD to confirm the plan for later that evening. His secretary said that he was too busy to speak but the agents would be picking them up between 9:30 and 10 that night. She added that Casey was arranging something special for that evening session and that he would brief them about it later.

CHAPTER 9

The Story of the Syrian

Adnan Bahar was a Syrian and was an honest, hardworking boatman of much experience. His father had always insisted that he should never become involved in politics, like so many other young men with passion and anger in their hearts.

'If you find that you have fire in your belly, then you use it for hard work, not for politics or violence. That way you will prosper, my son. The other way can easily destroy you,' he often reminded him.

When it was arranged for him to meet a girl with a view to marriage, he could not believe his good fortune. Her name was Maya and she was the most beautiful female he had ever seen. She was not only slim and very attractive but her father, a medical doctor, had educated her and she was an intelligent and serious person who simply captured his heart. It was not long before they married and eventually, when Maya gave birth to their son, it seemed that life could not be any better.

After some years had passed Adnan became aware

that good job opportunities were available for boatmen with experience to work for a river haulage company in Iraq. With his experience he secured the job and, along with his wife and Tarek, his son, he moved to Iraq to a town called ad-Dawr but later moved to better accommodation on the outskirts of al-Fathar, not far from the big River Tigris. Adnan had a small crew of two other men and regularly took produce on a barge north as far as al Mawsil and sometimes south down to Baghdad, always on the Tigris. He became very familiar with the area and as they had spare land with their little cottage Maya busied herself with some chickens and a few goats. Their life was good and they were very happy, but they had not reckoned with 'The Butcher of Baghdad.' Saddam Hussein was reputed to have been responsible for murdering more than 250,000 of his own people, not to mention the countless thousands of lives lost over the eight years of senseless war with Iran.

Saddam's elite troops, the Republican Guard, were not only better trained than the main regular army, but they were fiercely loyal and better paid. They received free housing and cars and they knew they were highly regarded by their egomaniac president who could never see any wrong in their frightful and often brutal behaviour.

One day Maya was at home with her seven-year-old son Tarek. She had been preparing a meal and was expecting Adnan to be home that afternoon having been away for three days. From her kitchen she could see the dust cloud of three military vehicles approaching the small holding. As they got closer, she recognised the markings of the Republican Guard and felt her stomach twist into a knot.

'Tarek! Tarek! Go out into the back yard into the chicken shed. Do it now, boy,' she called.

'Why, Mama? What is happening?' he answered. She quickly pushed the boy through into the back yard as the truck and two Land Rovers pulled up outside.

'Go and hide until the soldiers have gone,' she hissed.

The troops in the lorry stayed put but four soldiers got out of the two Land Rovers and for a few seconds brushed the dust from their uniforms before approaching the cottage.

Maya could pick out the one in charge, obviously an officer as he was dressed a bit differently to the others. *Why do these officer soldiers seem to copy the Hussein look?* she wondered. He was a sturdy man with a bit of a belly and had the typical Saddam moustache. He also wore a black beret and a side-arm on his belt.

He kicked open the door and arrogantly sauntered

in, closely followed by the three others. Without looking at Maya he slowly made his way around the cottage, checking each corner of the abode before returning to the kitchen. She kept her eyes averted as he came close to her and poked around at the food that she had prepared for her little family.

He picked up a piece of spiced chicken quarter from a tray that was on the table and started eating it. Maya stayed still and kept her eyes looking downwards. When he finished, he threw the bone at her and grabbed her by her arm and pulled her harshly towards him. He held her face tightly under the chin and stared at her for a few seconds before punching her to the side of her head and yelling, 'Shia whore! You filthy Shia whore!'

Maya dropped to the floor like a stone. Her head was spinning from the blow and she struggled to get up but suddenly felt her garments being ripped and cut from her body with a knife. She turned to look upwards and saw her aggressor preparing himself to rape her.

The adrenalin and horrific fear of what was about to happen filled her being and she suddenly leaped to her feet in an effort to escape. Another blow hit her hard in the mouth and nose and again, she fell to the floor. Two teeth had either snapped or come out, for she could feel them in her mouth and the blood from her nose and split lips caused her to cough and splutter.

The Saddam 'look-alike' dropped his weight onto her and she was aware of him holding a knife under her chin. There were voices in the room, jeering, laughing from the other men. She could feel someone pulling at her ankle, someone was helping this man. As the assault started she could not believe the brutality of the deed. The only man she had ever known, or hoped to know, was her loving Adnan. He was always so gentle with her, so caring and thoughtful. But this? This was nothing she could ever have imagined. It was the stuff of nightmares. She heard raised voices not far away.

The door still lay open and Maya looked outside. She could see half a dozen of the troops from the lorry surrounding Adnan and holding him by his shirt. She realised the horror of what was unfolding and screamed with all her might. Adnan lashed out at the man holding him and broke away but the others quickly grabbed him and forced him to the ground. He fought and struggled gallantly as he bellowed his wife's name loudly over and over. Maya became aware that her attacker had finished his deed and was now standing up and shouting to his men outside. She was also aware that she was shaking and crying but suddenly her eyes opened wide as a new horror gripped her. From the side of the building Tarek ran to his father screaming 'Papa! Papa! I'll help you!' The soldiers laughed and grabbed the boy roughly as he fought hard to reach his father.

Maya shouted to her son but before she could rise to her feet, another weight dropped upon her and she felt herself becoming the victim once again. Through the pain and horror of these events, she tried to close off her mind to this experience and watched the officer outside approaching Adnan and Tarek who were held firmly on the ground. He casually stood near them adjusting his beret on his head before removing his side-arm from its holster. He looked at his watch on his left wrist, then pointing the weapon downwards fired twice. He looked back towards the kitchen and shouted a command. Maya heard a great gasp from her attacker as he finished and, dressing hurriedly, he joined the others outside. Soon the vehicles started up and in a cloud of dust from the wheels the Republican Guard drove off at speed.

Maya did not move. She lay as if in a stupor. Her mouth open, her breathing shallow. Her nose blocked with congealing blood. She lay, mostly naked on the stone floor staring out onto the front yard of their happy, beautiful little cottage. The front yard where her seven-year-old son, her innocent little boy, and her hard-working, loving husband lay dead, both with a single bullet each to the head.

How long she laid there on the kitchen floor she could not say, but when she did finally get to her feet she was a totally different woman to the one who had been preparing a meal for her little family some time earlier. Her mind had gone numb and she felt a very strange and new sensation inside her. It was as if her heart had turned to stone and the only emotion or feeling that she could experience was one of indescribable hatred.

The Long Journey Forward

The days that passed were like a bad dream for Maya. Her life as she knew it had violently ended and now all she could consider was revenge. She knew very little about politics, she knew no one in this country who could help her and as a lone Syrian Shia woman living in Saddam Hussein's Iraq, she felt very vulnerable, so what was she to do? Each day that passed, this question became more and more important. At the graveside of Adnan and Tarek she made no prayer to Allah but what she did instead was to swear an oath in their memory that she would do everything in her power to avenge their deaths. Eventually a plan of some sort came into her mind. A plan that may seem impossible, but a plan that she would attempt to try...

The year was 2003 and America had started to invade Iraq. She knew that military activity was becoming intense, especially this close to Tikrit, Saddam's favourite place in the whole country. She simply had to get out and her stoical zeal pointed her towards the USA.

She enlisted the help of Adnan's colleagues from the barge who were outraged at the fate of their former friend. They hid her on the barge one day and took her north along the Tigris towards Turkey, while most military security was heavily involved with the spreading war further south near Baghdad. Among the few possessions she took with her was a folder of documents that she hoped would stand her in good stead when applying for asylum. Her marriage certificate was one and also the hospital form from Syria after she gave birth to Tarek.

Maya's journey to the USA and acceptance as an asylum seeker was a testament to her courage and determination, but her plan was not complete with that success. From the day of her acceptance she tried to involve herself in any way she could with the authorities. Her English language was quite passable and she tried repeatedly with the police department to act as an Arabic interpreter but with little success.

By now the coalition was achieving great success in Iraq and the country appeared jubilant at the removal of their tyrant dictator. The difficulty that beset the American government was that Saddam Hussein had disappeared and, despite a reward of $25 million, no one had come forward with any useful information. His two evil and cruel sons, Uday and Qusay Hussein had been killed in a building in Mosul during a shoot-out with American soldiers, but the dictator himself was nowhere to be found. President Bush knew that as long as Saddam was at large there was always a risk of a future resurgence and there was pressure throughout all military and enforcement departments to find him.

Maya constantly tried to make herself useful to the authorities and it was only when she mentioned one day to a police officer during one of her visits to the police station that she had lived near Tikrit and knew the area well that a bright young detective thought to pass on her details to the FBI. She was initially interviewed, assessed and logged into the system, but months went by without her being contacted again.

CHAPTER 10

Two New Code Names

J D had got to his office early with Maya to explain some details to her. It was not his intention to physically introduce the two main players in this event, that wasn't really necessary, but they would have to be aware of each other's presence in order for this to work.

Maya was already on file by the code name of 'Songbird' for her anonymity and protection. David was given the rather apt codename of 'Rip van Winkle.'

Some people might have thought it unwise to allow a Muslim to witness this Western man going through, what could be called, psychic espionage against Islam. However, the FBI chief was only too aware of Songbird's commitment to the downfall of Saddam and how she would do her utmost to advance that cause.

She was already seated in the little observation room when David and Jenny arrived that evening. No mention was made of the altercation of that morning but instead JD went straight into an explanation of his plan with 'Songbird.' It was very much, 'Let's do business!'

Now aware that they could be seen in the main bedroom via the two-way mirror, they both changed into their night clothes in the en-suite. David got into bed on his side and Jenny pulled up the easy chair close to his pillow. For reassurance he studied, once again, the picture of Saddam for several seconds before laying back and getting settled.

About two or three minutes passed in silence as David drifted into a relaxed, drowsy state. He mentioned the bar of light and that it was still slow but not as slow as it had been the day previous. As the eyes became clearer and larger, once again, they slowed right down and then, at that split second of merging with David's own vision, he gave a small, almost imperceptible convulsion of the body. His eyes were closed and he suddenly grimaced before stating loudly, 'Saddam is here and he is very angry. He is with two men and he is shouting at them. These men are subdued and appear to me to be scared. They are back in the same little room as last time. I will leave them and go outside if I can, to try and see some landmarks.' He was doing well tonight and appreciated the urgency of finding a proper location. 'I am going up... up... higher, and looking down.

This room, or hut really, seems part of a derelict farm. The rest looks burnt out. We are not too far from a substantial river.'

Songbird was staring at David with eyes like saucers. 'Ask him to look at the river. Look at the banks. What can he tell us about it?' she urged JD. She could hear through her own set of headphones what was taking place in the next room, but only JD could speak to Jenny.

JD repeated the request to Jenny. 'Long reeds. Thousands of them. They run far along the embankments. Some have fluffy white tops on them. I can see some big barges on the river. They have Arab writing on the sides and are painted yellow and green.' His voice was husky and he spoke slowly. Songbird stood up in the control room and turned to JD. 'Ask him if the barges have blue flags on the rail at the rear.' This was duly passed on.

'Yes, they have. Both of them. I am going higher now so I can see further. Wait. Wait a minute. Those two men who were in the hut just now are outside and they are pulling at a dirty old rug that is lying on the ground not far away. They are brushing away the dirt and there is a trap door under the old rug! This is near the edge of an orange grove. One of them has lifted up the trap door and I can see a wooden ladder going down into some kind of dug out chamber below. This has to be a secret hiding hole. I'm going down into the chamber to see what is stored there. I can tell you it is deep enough for a man to stand upright. One of these men is carrying a bundle down the ladder. It could be a blanket or two, not sure. At the bottom it widens out a bit but it's not high. You would have to lie down. About a metre high. There is an electric cable down here that is connected to a neon strip light and also a fan. It's getting dark in here now. The light is fading. It's getting weaker.' Then there was silence.

JD glanced at Songbird. She was staring through the glass and her mouth hung open. 'Was he supposed to be with Saddam Hussein as he is now, or was he just imagining that he was?' she asked incredulously.

'Well, it appears to us that he was actually at the same place as Hussein at this moment. Wherever that place may be.'

'Oh. That was Iraq, and that river is the Tigris.' She was nodding her head and rubbing her hands together. 'He talked about the barges and unless he has lived there, he would not have known about the colours or the flags. This is my region and I know it. Is this Englishman coming back? We cannot stop now!' She sounded excited and desperate at the same time.

The next day dragged by so slowly for the Sorensens. They too felt so close to finding the target. They phoned up agent Leoni, as promised, and stated their wish to go to the shopping mall. She, in turn, phoned up a reliable taxi service for them and followed them when they reached the mall. They tried to see if they could spot her following them, but she was too good to stand out in the crowd and they never saw her. Eventually they got fed up with wandering around and took a yellow cab back home. As they paid off the driver, Agent Leoni drove past their house and returned to base. They tried to relax in the afternoon but all the time both of them kept thinking that tonight could be the night they find the location, and they remained quiet and lost in their own thoughts. Pick up time was for 9pm. and after a brief chat with JD they could settle down for another evening of hopeful revelation.

Songbird had taken up position in the other room again by the time the Sorensens had arrived. She was nothing if not dedicated to this project. For the first time since her devastating experience she could feel some sense of hope. She had slept very little and was hoping against all odds that this strange Englishman with his strange dream talk could bring to justice the monster who murdered her family and killed her soul.

To her thinking, David was some kind of magician who could perform powerful magic. She wondered if it could ever be possible for him to find the officer who had raped her.

As usual David slipped into his drowsy state quite easily, but the eyes took several anxious minutes before they appeared on the scene. It was daytime in Iraq of course, and David's commentary went straight to Saddam. This time he was washing himself down from a large water bowl in the hut, so without any instructions David appeared to direct his vision speedily outside, back towards the river and went upwards. His vision went far.

'I can see a main road now, more like a motorway, not so far from the river and it leads off towards a town. This old abandoned farm is one of two and they are on the east bank. There is an orange grove at the one that Saddam is hiding in, but it's old and neglected.'

Songbird stood up suddenly and shouted, 'I know! I know! That road is called the 24 and I lived at Al-Awja; but he is talking about a small place called ad-Dawr. Send your troops there. Go there! You will find these two farms, they are the only ones there. If this man Rip Winki is right, then The Butcher is hiding in one of those two old farms, but I do not

95

know of this orange grove. It may be there somewhere but I don't know which one.'

JD felt a strange excitement and left the control room to return to his office. Anything further that David had to say would be recorded but for now he had to look at his detailed map of Iraq. There he found it, almost imperceptibly small, but there, nevertheless. A tiny little area called ad-Dawr. He swiftly placed a coded call to the White House and spoke to the senior duty officer and asked him to pass on directly to the president the information he had just gleaned, with apologies for the unavoidably late hour. The sequence of progress would now come from orders given to the US military working in that area.

CHAPTER 11

Saddam Hussein had been missing without trace for nine months. There had been various intel reports and during that time the military had carried out no less than twelve hard-hitting raids at different locations but without success. They always went in force as it was believed that there would be a heavy resistance from his Republican Guard.

From the White House to the military chiefs in Iraq came the orders for the search of the area as given by David and Songbird. Maps were studied and the approximate locations of the farms were determined. This operation was to be called Operation Red Dawn and the two farms were to be identified as Wolverine One and Wolverine Two. A large number of troops were mustered, briefed and mobilised.

The whole area of the two farms was surrounded and as the cordon closed in tighter and tighter, not only was there an absence of people but not a single shot was fired. When they came upon Wolverine Two they found a couple of Iraqi civilians sitting in the cluttered little hut, but they made no attempt to resist the US troops. The army colonel in charge suddenly noticed a small overgrown orange grove nearby and concentrated his attention around it. As the troops slowly commenced their search, one of them noticed a dirty old rug lying in the dust. Beneath that rug was a thick polystyrene block that was level with the ground and beneath that was the hole where Saddam Hussein, the once illustrious president of Iraq was hiding in squalid conditions.

Although he carried a side-arm, he made no attempt to use it and surrendered the instant he was discovered. He was in possession of 750,000 US dollars.

President Bush was jubilant and personally congratulated JD for his success with Operation Eagle Eye. The truth of the operation could never really be revealed without putting the English couple into the spotlight, so JD thought up a perfectly believable story of how a close confidante of Saddam's and another captured former member of the Ba'ath Party had given the vital information. The story was accepted without question and everyone was just happy with the successful conclusion. The whole media storm now moved on to Saddam's trial, sentence and eventual execution. Everything seemed to have gone so well and JD Casey's efforts were considered 'Golden.' Except for one little thing.

An ecstatic Syrian woman called Maya Bahar,

AKA 'Songbird.'

The Rewards

Next morning the Sorensens were taken home by the two agents but they never saw JD.

He left a message for them to rest up and take things easy and that he would be in touch very soon. They actually learned of Saddam's arrest from the television when President Bush addressed the nation and they saw the live footage of the fugitive being taken from his hideout. For David and Jenny it seemed a bit of an anti-climax and they had a feeling of being ignored. The television news channels were full of the Iraq report but not a lot more was to be learned so they switched it off.

By late afternoon JD Casey telephoned Jenny's mobile and asked if it was convenient to visit them both with some important news. He arrived an hour later and greeted them like long-lost relatives. He shook their hands and hugged Jenny and accepted their offer of a black coffee before settling down into an armchair with a file of papers on his lap.

'Because you are a "secret" the president thanks you, through me, for your outstanding help and has authorised the release of the allotted reward money, which neatly brings me on to my next subject. Songbird. As you will appreciate, David, her input was definitely useful and time saving because of her geographical knowledge. The reward stands at $25 million and I feel strongly that she deserves a slice of the action. How does $20 million for you and $5 million for her sound? Is that fair?'

'Yes. Of course. That sounds fair. Will I be meeting her at some stage?' David asked.

'No. There is no need for that, although she has seen you and Jenny through the glass. I don't want you all becoming best buddies or anything. Remember one thing, that the help you have given Uncle Sam would make you many enemies in some areas. You must think "security" at all times. Now then, what are your immediate plans? I realise that your "period of ability" is almost finished for this year. With your new-found wealth and government-approved freedom to stay in the USA you can disappear somewhere peaceful and beautiful until we can pick up the thread again in eleven months. Is that about right? There will always be work for you to do, always problems for your particular ability to tackle. What do you say?' JD sounded eager for David's approval of his suggestion.

'We would like to return home as soon as possible. Jenny's mother lives alone and Christmas is around the corner. We always have Christmas and New Year together, so I think it suits us better to get back to England really soon. We can always come back again next year, early enough for a fresh start with the guiding eyes,' David replied.

JD's facial expression changed to a frown. He suddenly looked disappointed. 'I was hoping you were going to stay. Mainly because it presents an embarrassing situation, which is really an IRS problem but it affects you both. You see, the reward money must go into your American account, that's no problem, but it must stay in the country for one year before it can be accessed abroad. In other words, if you go back to Britain as planned then you won't be able to use any of the reward money for a year. Will that cause a big problem for you? These are regulations, I'm afraid.' He sounded sincere but, of course, he was lying.

'Well, it's not what we expected. We had no idea we had to leave the money here. It seems odd that we were not told this before now,' Jenny replied.

'Heck. I'm sorry about this. I didn't know about it myself until today. But listen. How about bringing Jenny's mum over here for Christmas and New Year?

You can afford to fly her first class now and it would be a real change for her. You will have to move out of the safe house very soon, now that operation Eagle Eye has finished, so you can use a couple of days finding a real good furnished place to rent to give you some breathing space. You will disappear off the radar, live a quiet life until we can pick up, like I said, in about eleven months' time. It's just an alternative for you to consider, that's all.'

'Do we say goodbye to our security guys?' asked David.

JD nodded. 'Well, sure you do. You're not in a witness protection program. Once the operation has finished you go back to living a normal, quiet life somewhere and don't ever talk about the operation or your involvement in it to anyone.'

The idea seemed sound and they went along with it. A first-class ticket was bought for Brenda, Jenny's mum, who was thrilled at the idea of seeing a bit of the USA. It also gave the Sorensens a bit of time with a realtor to find a suitable temporary property to rent, until they were absolutely sure where they wanted to buy.

They soon found a recently built, four-bedroomed house just outside the town of Monterey, on the west coast of California. It was a property with a large front drive, with a circular raised flower bed. A solid, six-foot-high wall ran around the perimeter of the property and the front was accessed via large, electrically operated gates.

David knew that the security was not up to the standard of the safe house in Washington, but Monterey on the west coast was nearly three thousand road miles from the capital, right over on the east side. They had decided to rent the house on a renewable six-month contract and felt safe in their anonymity.

For Brenda, leaving her little cottage in Surrey to fly to the USA, was a big adventure, especially travelling first class. Her group of friends at Whitely Village waved her goodbye and enviously wished her Bon Voyage. Everything went smoothly for her and she was really impressed with the house that David and Jenny were renting. On Christmas Day David revealed their wish for her to live with them in America where they would love her company and to include her into their lives. She was deeply touched by the offer but had to refuse. 'I think I'm too old to start life afresh, my dears, and oh, how I'd miss the old gang back home. Anyway, I don't speak the language here!'

They all laughed but then Jenny spoke. 'Seriously, Mum. If we were to decide to stay here permanently, we would feel bad about abandoning you so far away.

Please reconsider.'

'Listen,' Brenda replied, 'you will not be abandoning me at all. We can speak regularly on the phone and you can teach me to use the web-cam gadget on the computer so we can always be close. Besides, coming here has been such an adventure and I would love to be able to do it again, maybe in the summer?' She seemed animated by the idea and they agreed.

Christmas was a happy time for the three of them and all too soon Brenda was taken to the airport for her return journey back home, back to her peaceful, quiet little village life.

CHAPTER 12

Maya lived in a small Muslim community, many of whom were refugees of some kind. She was poor and eked out a living by serving in a shop that sold eastern spices. She was only required for four hours a day but was needed seven days a week. Her community knew of her background in Iraq as well as her hatred for the regime and felt genuine pity for her. Suddenly, one day, almost overnight, she became very wealthy. She gave up her job, of course, and bought an apartment not far from where she had lived before. She didn't want to lose contact with the few friends she had in this country and decided to have a party for them and to show off her new home.

Whether she was so full of excitement and boasting about her part in locating Saddam, or whether she was pressured into explaining where her new-found wealth had come from, no one really knew, but she blurted out the whole story to an amazed audience. She spoke in great detail about the Englishman and his wife who could travel in their sleep to any part of the world and find you and report back about what you were doing and where you were living. It made a good story and her popularity naturally grew. She was generous to her new asylum friends and, flattered by the attention that she attracted, her account of Saddam's capture grew more incredible with every telling.

Her burning mission in life had been achieved and her part in it had been handsomely rewarded. She was a contented woman and had no wish to cause difficulties for the English couple, but her story travelled far and what should have remained a secret was now becoming known to too many. Not all the Muslim community had identical sympathies and soon those of a different persuasion, heard of her experience.

A Sleeper Awakens

Supporters of terrorism exist everywhere, and sleepers integrate with society just waiting for instructions that may never come. But for Hamid Raisani that day did come, and the plan was very simple. The briefcase contained explosives with a basic spring-loaded detonator attached to the handle. From the detonator would come a thin wire and if pulled it would release the spring and the bomb would explode. It was simple but effective.

Minimum surveillance showed Raisani that the Englishman always drove his car into his driveway going left of the circular flower bed, probably a habit from his years of driving in the UK. He occasionally left the car parked at the front of the house, thinking that the electric gates and high wall were sufficient to keep outsiders away. Mostly it was garaged overnight.

It took four passing night checks in his car for Raisani to strike it lucky. By midnight on the fifth day the Sorensen house was in darkness and now, at last, the SUV was parked in the driveway, not far from the front door. He parked fifty yards away from the house and slipped out of his car with the briefcase and a roll of thin wire. Dressed in black with a dark woollen hat covering his bald head he was almost invisible on this moonless winter's night. He carefully placed the briefcase on top of the front wall and managed to climb up beside it. He jumped down into the shrubbery of the front garden and lay close to the ground for several minutes. There was not a sound, nor did any light come on. When he felt safe to continue, he stood up, reached carefully for the case and bent double, approached the car. Taking the roll of thin wire from his pocket he attached one end securely to the front bumper. He then passed the roll of wire under the car and slipped the case containing the explosives, along the ground beneath the driver's seat. The last thing, was to take a small pair of pliers from his pocket and cut off the excess wire, allowing himself just enough to connect to the ring of the detonator that hung proud of the case. As the car would move forward the wire would pull out the spring clip and the bomb would take this infidel devil back to his hell and another victory for Allah would have been achieved.

The whole operation took only eleven minutes and Raisani was soon back in his car and reporting to his master on his mobile phone with a simple code word to indicate that the job had been completed successfully.

CHAPTER 13

The euphoria of Saddam's arrest soon faded as other important things arose in the FBI, but JD Casey found himself thinking about the experience he had had with the Sorensens. As the project had closed, he withdrew the close security, released the reward money, with strings attached and sent the naive, but pleasant couple out into the open on their own. He hadn't even shown much interest, other than getting their address in Monterey, or sending someone to check that their new premises were secure. His conscience bothered him a bit but he told himself that Monterey was thousands of miles away and they would be two unknowns in the area. They should be fine and anyway, if they felt uncomfortable with anything, they always had his direct number that they could call. That much he did afford them.

The Shopping List

Jenny woke up that morning with a thumping headache. They had eaten out the previous night and apart from the one glass of red wine that David drank, she finished the bottle. 'I'm not looking for sympathy but that wine was so good last night I just couldn't leave it. Now I've got a headache!' she moaned over breakfast.

'That's OK. Why don't you take a couple of tablets and go back to bed? Best cure. I can do the grocery run on my own.'

'No. No. Leave it until tomorrow and we can go together then.'

'Jen, I can do the shopping by myself. It doesn't need two of us. Besides, we haven't got much in the way of dinner for tonight anyway. You take a nap and I'll be back in a couple of hours. I'll bring you up a cup of tea when I get back, OK? See how you are then.'

She smiled and nodded gratefully. 'Thank you so much. I'll get the shopping list.'

David took the keys from the hall cupboard and left the house. Just as he started up the SUV he could hear Jenny shouting from the doorstep.

'You've forgotten the shopping list!' She was beckoning him to drop back a few feet so she could hand it to him through the driver's window. He laughed and selecting reverse, he drove backwards to line up with Jenny. The bomb, instead of being under the driver's seat, was now about three feet in front of the bumper as the sprung pin pulled out of the detonator.

The blast pushed Jenny off her feet and back into the hall. The front of the SUV lifted up and, being in reverse anyway, it shot back about five yards. The whole front of the vehicle was destroyed, tyres, windscreen, engine all ripped apart, and how David was not killed, can only be accredited to the robust passenger compartment. Fortunately, the fuel tank was at the rear and being a diesel vehicle, was not so inflammable, otherwise the whole car could have become an inferno.

David had been half turned in his seat when the bomb went off and his injuries came mostly from the flying debris as the windscreen disintegrated. His right shoulder was badly torn open and the side of his head was pouring with blood. He lay unconscious, slumped against the driver's door, his ears now deaf to any surrounding sounds. Jenny could also hear nothing and although her hands were shaking, she controlled her voice as she spoke to the operator on 911 repeating over and over, the words, ambulance, bomb explosion, deafness and then address. She did that about four times before she dropped the phone and ran back out to David. She knew she should not try and move him but she grabbed a clean towel from the house and climbing onto the front passenger seat she folded it and held it against his bleeding head.

The tears ran down her face at the thought of losing this man whom she loved. She was not a person who prayed often but now the words flowed quickly from her trembling lips as she pleaded with God to spare her husband.

Two police cars arrived first but could not get in immediately because of the locked gates.

Jenny could not hear their shouts or their sirens and had not realised that anyone had arrived until one young officer managed to scramble over the wall and run up to her. She fell into his arms in floods of tears and started shaking uncontrollably. Soon the gates had been opened and the ambulance arrived and the crime scene was properly managed. Fortunately, the house was not damaged and ensuring that the front door was locked, and that Jenny had the keys, they took both her and David to hospital. The police officers kept the remote control for the gates as the remains of the SUV would need to be removed for examination. Although there was very little hope of finding any DNA on it they still had to fingerprint the outside of the car, in case the perpetrator had touched it when placing the explosives.

While David was in the operating theatre, Jenny

was checked for any injury. She was treated for shock and being sedated, soon fell asleep in an armchair in a side room.

Two weeks had gone by and the Sorensens, now back in their house, had not ventured out once. The trauma of the whole incident had shocked and frightened them greatly. It was not easy to grasp that there were people out there who wanted them dead and were fully capable of making that happen. They ordered their groceries to be delivered and often they would have take-away meals brought to them, for there was no desire to go out.

David's arm was heavily bandaged and in a sling and the injury to his face and head was quite bad. Healing would obviously take time and his face would need further ongoing treatments. Eventually plastic surgery would be required, but not for some considerable time yet.

The pain he was experiencing was great and the hospital had given him strong medication which they thought he would be taking for weeks to come. Their house phone very rarely rang and this time, when it did, Jenny cautiously answered the phone with a simple, 'Yes?'

'Hi Jenny. It's JD. I've just flown in from

Washington and I'm in Monterey right now. I'd like to come and see you both. Will that be convenient?'

She remained silent.

'I mean, if it's not good right now then maybe tomorrow some time?' he asked.

'Have you heard about the assassination attempt on David's life, or is this just a social call?' Her voice was ice cold and she waited for his reply.

'Yeah, of course. That's why I'm here. I have some news for you apart from wanting to see you again and offer my sympathies and help in any way that I can.'

'The attempted murder was fifteen days ago, Mr. Casey. Been busy, have you?'

He could feel the tension in her voice and knew he needed to be cautious.

'I did hear about it at the time and if you think I have been negligent in communication then I apologise, Jenny. Truth is, it's because of our work together that this has happened and I didn't think you would want to hear from me while things were so raw and fresh in your minds. I felt a little healing break was necessary before speaking to you, and then I thought, "Hell no, I'm going to fly out there and see them in person!"' He tried to sound upbeat.

'That's very magnanimous, Mr. Casey. You can come now if you wish. We are doing nothing that can't wait.'

'That's good and I'm looking forward to seeing you both again. How long has it been?'

'About three months or more. Why?'

'Well, in three months or more I am still JD, OK? What's with the "Mr. Casey" anyway?'

'See you soon. Goodbye.' She clicked off the phone before he could say another word. Jenny Sorensen was in no mood to roll over for anyone. Not now. Not ever again.

Reverse Decision

David was drowsy from the tablets and struggled to keep his eyes open, but his wife was sharp as ever. JD sat opposite them both with a black coffee in his hand and appeared relaxed.

'We cannot be sure, but your identity may have been accidentally leaked by "Songbird." Inadvertently, while bragging about her achievement of finding Saddam, she may well have told about the Englishman with strange powers of detection. Stories travel fast and the wrong ears get to hear them. It was only last weekend, Sunday actually, that I learned of the sudden death of Maya Bahar, AKA "Songbird", who allegedly fell from the balcony of her new home onto a paved courtyard. Suffered massively from depression apparently after horrific events in Iraq. Suspected suicide. Death was from severe cranial trauma.' He paused and looked up at the ceiling for some seconds before adding, 'Strange how the fatal injury was more consistent with that of a hammer head than a paving stone. I knew then that Operation Eagle Eye had been compromised. I am so sorry. I am genuinely sorry.'

David had been staring at him with half-open eyes. He waved his good hand in a dismissive manner and shook his head. His voice was weak and croaky. 'Not your fault, old boy. No blame. Thank you for coming to see us.'

JD looked at the other man, head and one eye heavily bandaged, one arm in a sling and thought how close he had come to death. His sorrow was genuine.

'I am sending a top security guy over soon to advise you. You certainly need approach lights front and back. You need CCTV with night vision, you need panic alarms. Hell, David, you need the works. Now my second bit of news is this. Your money is now unlocked. It's yours no matter what. That is official. What do you have to say about that, eh?'

David was asleep, slumped in his armchair but

Jenny spoke out.

'That is good news indeed about freeing up the American account, thank you for that. Do not worry about your security guy. This is rented property, don't forget, and we can't just let rip with alterations. Besides, if our money is really ours to do with as we please then we will very soon be returning home to England. David needs further ongoing treatment and yes, there are brilliant doctors in America, but we would prefer to get that treatment back home.'

JD nodded and stared down at his now cold coffee. He was thinking how the Director had praised him for his work on Operation Eagle Eye, but now his 'prized asset' from the UK should be made available for the CIA. Their tasks regarding national security at this time were paramount. He argued forcibly against this decision but finally was ordered directly to hand over his file on the Sorensen story.

Some days later someone from the Agency called to ask if he had finished with Songbird.

'Yeah, I guess so. She was a low-level asset and I tried using her in an experiment which paid off in aces, but as far as I'm concerned, she is no longer useful to me. Why do you ask?'

There was a long pause before the agent replied. 'Seems to me she's a liability. Dangerous, even. This particular songbird should stop singing.' The phone call ended.

About a week later JD heard about Maya's untimely death.

thing he ever wanted was publicity or any form of notoriety. He did say that his accident had occurred in America which would explain why Adam, or anybody else for that matter, hadn't seen the report in any British newspaper.

David's treatment would involve several visits to the hospital at spaced intervals, for each procedure to heal before continuing with the next. Adam and his wife lived in Epsom in Surrey, not very distant from David's Twickenham address. Before the two men said farewell they exchanged phone details and agreed to meet up sometime for a meal or a drink.

The Sagittarius Time

As November went by, the Sorensens were only too aware that the guiding eyes would quite probably be returning should David follow the procedure as before. This past year had been a traumatic time for them both and Jenny was most apprehensive about David working again, with any kind of professional agency. She never mentioned anything to him about her feelings in the hope that they could forget about it and go back to how things were before.

One morning, at the beginning of December,

David confided in his wife during breakfast.

'Jen, last night I tried with the eyes. There was an article in the local paper with a picture of the lord mayor opening some function or another. I studied his face thoroughly and then drifted off into space. Guess what? Nada! Absolutely nothing. Eventually I just went to sleep. I didn't even think about the mayor in my sleep. Weird, or what?'

'I've never said this before, David, but I'm relieved in a big way. I almost saw you murdered in Monterey and I don't ever want to see that again. It's not the "ability" that scares me, it's how it can be applied to tracing bad people. That's my main worry! If those bad people find out what you can do then they will come after you like they did in America.'

He could see her concern and accepted that she had good cause to be. The explosion had been a nightmare and it was not over yet, not with several more painful medical procedures still lined up. If that phenomenon ever came back to him, he would be ultra-cautious. That's for sure.

He tried it again about a week later and again there was no result, no image, nothing.

Christmas was a week away and according to his star sign theory the ability should cease on or around December 23rd. During that week he studied various faces before bedtime every night and it became obvious to him that the ability that had come suddenly into his life had just as suddenly deserted him. He wasn't angry about it, but he was a bit perplexed by it all because he couldn't truthfully explain where it came from.

David and Jenny had met up once or twice with the policeman Adam and his wife, Gillian. Adam always had such interesting stories to relate about crime and criminals and arrests and David's life, in comparison, had been very routine, almost mundane. Except, of course, for his ability and the Saddam story in America. That was now in the past. The ability had gone and most likely would not be coming back, so David figured there would be no harm in telling Adam all about it. It would be the sort of story that he would appreciate and possibly he may have even come across something similar in his line of work.

Yes, Adam was totally fascinated by the story and no, he had never heard of the like. 'Where's it coming from, David?' he asked. 'Are you some sort of psychic? Do you hear voices and can you speak to these eyes at any stage?'

'I wish I knew myself,' he replied. 'No, I haven't spoken to the eyes really. It's as if they know anyway what I want to do, and they sort of lead the way. I did feel very comfortable when they were with me. Not afraid or anything. It was really a very unusual but good kind of experience. I always felt that it was meant to be used positively and not treated as a stage show for magicians. Not that it ever was, of course, although I did have to be tested at times.'

'If it ever came to you again, would you use it for the purpose of good? I mean, if your answer is no, then what's it all about?'

'Good point, Adam. I suppose whatever "it" is, it does need to be cultivated. As you say, what would be the purpose of it in the first place, eh?'

Adam swore that he would never repeat David's story or reveal his true identity to anyone without David's specific permission or request.

Time passed by and at this point they had been back in the UK for eighteen months. Summer was now upon them and life was relaxed and comfortable and they would claim to have 'taken early retirement' to anyone who should ask them.

The Sorensens weren't just financially comfortable, they were fairly wealthy by anyone's standards. The 20 million US dollars translated into well over 15 million sterling, so there were no money worries at all. Jenny went back to her art classes and she always loved her crafting hobby also, making beautiful greetings cards.

Adam was a keen golfer and offered to take David under his wing, teach him the basics and sponsor him for club membership.

The Eyes Return

They had been to Wembley Arena to see their favourite musical band. They were not disappointed and felt very uplifted by the whole evening's entertainment. The lead singer, in particular, had such a good voice and charisma. It was an excellent evening's entertainment. In bed David was thinking about the show and reliving his favourite bits when, to his total amazement, he saw the familiar distant band of bright light, like a phosphorous bar burning in the dark. He could feel his pulse racing with anticipation as it approached him. It was so long since he had last experienced this phenomenon and he wondered if anything would be different. As the bar of light stopped a few feet away from him he recognised that within it were the same eyes staring, unblinking as before, looking at him intently.

The surrounding light diminished, as before, and the eyes became an intense bright green.

David was smiling now, as if he had met an old

friend and unconsciously, he softly said, 'Hello.'

Immediately the eyes closed for a couple of seconds and when they opened, although still unblinking they appeared to soften somehow. He thought that it was some sort of acknowledgement and he felt a strange surge of joy, but maybe it was just wishful thinking. Very slowly the eyes inched forward and just at the point of touching him David gave an involuntary shudder followed by extreme clarity of vision. What he suddenly now saw surprised him greatly, for lying unconscious on a floor with two paramedics attending to him, was the lead singer, the front man from tonight's band. He watched as they put him on a stretcher and, with help from two others from the band, they carried him out to the waiting ambulance.

David just could not accept this really because it was only a few hours ago that he and Jenny had seen this man in full swing at a brilliant show. He now felt silly because he thought that he was hallucinating by bringing the performer into his dream state. He forced himself awake and opening his eyes he took a drink of water from the glass on his bedside table.

When he drifted off to sleep again there was no sign of the guiding eyes. In the morning, as usual, he switched on the wall-mounted television as he sat down to breakfast at the kitchen table. The sound was low, but he saw the headlines of a tabloid newspaper on a news channel. The words seemed to jump out at him.

'Musician collapses at party following a sell-out Wembley performance. Dead on arrival at hospital.'

David knew it was back. It had all started up again and he felt a knot in his stomach. Jenny obviously knew but who else could he confide in? He desperately wanted to discuss the matter with someone and Adam was his only hope. He phoned him and told him what had happened and in order to talk about it in privacy they decided to book the golf course for a short but early round.

CHAPTER 15

Their standard of golf that day was abysmal, considering it was only nine holes. Their concentration just wasn't on the game as David related the events of last night's experience.

'Do you trust me?' Adam asked. 'I mean, trust me to protect you at all costs?'

David nodded. 'Yes, I do. Why do you ask?'

'I don't need to test you like the Americans did. I have no need to make you jump through any hoops to prove anything. In my line of work, David, your ability, your gift, your talent, call it what you like, would be very useful. To be able to trace someone, some fugitive for example, would be a great benefit for justice. It would be using the "ability" for the purpose of good, don't you think? And what if someone has been killed but there's no body? Do you think you would be able to locate them then?'

'Now that's something I have not tried. I would need to be tested on that count. I don't know about dead bodies. Supposing you asked where Jesus was buried, do you think that's going to work?' David took a swipe at the ball and missed it completely.

'I thought you said this all started when your brother was killed in a road accident?'

'Yes, I did. But apparently, he actually died at the hospital. Although fatally injured in the crash he didn't die until a little later. I just don't know, Adam. Maybe you can test me on that one, OK?'

Adam agreed and they made their way back to the club house.

A Journey into Possibilities

It was far too early for Adam, who by now was back at work, to even consider using David for police work. Not until he could trust the outcome of any information that he should receive. In his line of work quality of evidence was always paramount.

With regards to suspected murders, where the body was absent, he wondered if David could be of some use in that instance. He first tried him with a couple of photographs of people he knew to be dead but did not mention that fact. Strange for David, the eyes made no appearance after studying the photos one at a time on alternative nights. It became apparent to them both, when Adam revealed his actions, that this wasn't going to work with locating the bodies of dead people. One possible use would be locating missing or kidnapped people. That would be a plus. Then there would be the most obvious examples; fugitives, escaped prisoners and known suspected people who had moved away but were wanted for questioning regarding criminal matters. Adam could envisage many scenarios where David's abilities could be invaluable. But for identifying a perpetrator of crime when there were no suspects? No. David could not be useful then. Not really. His skill should be honed into identifying a certain location from the visions given to him through 'The Eyes'.

'How will you explain to your seniors where your information actually comes from, and how come it turns out to be so accurate?' David queried.

'They don't ask when it's accurate. They just get mad when it goes horribly wrong. I will simply say my info comes from a reliable and protected source if anyone should ask. I will always protect you, trust me. You will, forevermore be incognito.'

'That's how it must always be, Adam. It's for my own safety. You promise me anonymity and we've got a deal, OK? Jenny doesn't know about this yet. I hope she is going to be fine about it. At least the stakes are not as high as they were in America,' David replied seriously, still wondering how it all unravelled for him back then and how he became exposed.

The plastic surgery had been very good indeed, but every time he looked at himself in the mirror he could see the tell-tale change to his face and the faint scarring that was his legacy of helping to find Saddam Hussein. This sort of work obviously had its risks and, in some strange way, he knew that he must have been selected for this to happen to him. He accepted that if this was the truth then there simply had to be a purpose behind it. That is how he was going to explain it to Jenny and he crossed his fingers in the hope that she would buy into it. He need not have worried. When he told her everything and brought her up to speed, Jenny believed like he did, that this weird ability had been made possible for a reason, and that reason was for it to be used for a good purpose. That purpose didn't take long in coming.

Quality of Evidence

The Range Rover had cost him £50,000 and was silver-grey when he bought it a few months previously. It was quite legally registered in his name of Mr. Alexander Caulfield, but what wasn't legal was that he had it re-sprayed a vibrant mid-blue colour without informing the DVLA. If he was ever challenged regarding the colour, he would say that his favourite football team was Everton and this blue was the club colour. Not informing the DVLA was a complete oversight and he would get it done as soon as possible. A minor infringement.

What was also illegal, were the number plates front and rear for the sole purpose of avoiding CCTV or police camera recognition. The falsified number plates could now be identified as belonging to a blue Range Rover, same model, same year, legally registered to someone in some other part of the country.

Alex 'Buster' Caulfield was a hardened career criminal with a quick and violent temper.

The alteration to his car was just one of many schemes he undertook to avoid detection from the police. He had experienced just about everything that a life of crime has to offer and in the underworld was known as a 'big player.' His armed robbery gang was notable for their scary Halloween masks and easily discharged shotguns, bringing total fear to their victims.

He enjoyed the trappings of wealth that crime can sometimes supply, but he also had several visits to Her Majesty's prisons along the way. His preferred weapon of choice was a .38 calibre revolver, mainly because it left no shell casings behind after it was fired. The gun was secreted in a fixed holster beneath the dashboard, out of immediate sight, with the butt facing outwards for quick and easy access should an emergency arise.

He had picked up two shotguns with shortened barrels and pistol grip stocks with five boxes of shells to go with them. He had paid in cash and the criminal arms dealer from St. Albans had thrown in a box of twenty .38 calibre rounds for good measure. The bundle was wrapped up tightly in a tarpaulin in his boot and he felt in a good mood with his purchase. On his way back southwards to his house in Cobham, Surrey, he joined the M25 and became annoyed with the slow-moving Sunday traffic. He flashed his headlights and blasted the horn at anything in front of him that travelled less than ninety miles per hour. Suddenly a good stretch of road opened in front of him and he put his foot down to 110mph. The next vehicle up ahead was about four hundred yards away travelling fast, but slower than the Range Rover. Caulfield flashed his lights and the car immediately pulled into the centre lane. As he shot past it, he noticed that it was a powerful sports car and it instantly pulled out and tucked in behind him. He thought maybe some guy fancied a race, so he put his foot down some more and took it to 120mph. The car behind never left his tail and suddenly in his rear-view mirror he saw the blue flashing light on the roof. Although the car was an unmarked police car, the two guys in it were in uniform and were now wearing their hats and the passenger was pointing repeatedly to pull over. Caulfield had to think quickly. This was crazy. The last thing he wanted today was the police poking their noses into his car.

He knew there was no way he could outrun the police vehicle, even if the M25 gave him the opportunity to do so, which it rarely ever did.

As he eased right down and made his way across to the nearside lane, he noticed that not far up ahead was a slip road off the motorway with farm fields on the near side. He stretched his arm out of the window and pointed over the roof, at the same time indicating left.

The police car did likewise and stuck with him closely. He did not stop immediately but instead he continued along the slip-road for several hundred yards at a slow speed with his hazard lights on. The officers following, wondered what the idiot was doing. Suddenly, the Range Rover pulled into a farmer's field and came to a halt about 60 yards from the open gate. One officer approached the Range Rover while the other remained in the vehicle making checks on the police radio.

'Please step out of your vehicle and hand me the keys. I wish to speak to you.'

Caulfield pretended to look contrite. 'I know exactly what you must be thinking, Officer, and I apologise for my speeding. I had a call and my wife has collapsed while shopping and is in Kingston hospital. That's all I know so far and I am in a desperate hurry, but I am sorry.'

The policeman was unrelenting. 'Please step out of the car. We will make a few checks first, you will be reported for excess speed and then you can be on your way. Are you carrying anything in this vehicle?'

'Carrying anything? Oh, no. It's empty. I'm just in a hurry to get to my wife. For God's sake, man, can't you see I'm upset?'

'We will be as quick as possible, sir. We have a job to do and if you cooperate it will soon be completed.' The second policeman now left his car and was holding an open notebook with details of the owner of the fake number plates. He was heading towards the Range Rover and Caulfield knew the game was up. They would discover the number plate discrepancy, search his car and he would soon be back in prison for a long stretch. He realised all this in a heartbeat. These two assholes had to go.

'OK. You win. I'll get out.' The officer stepped

back from the Range Rover as Caulfield opened the door. He casually lifted his arm and just as it registered on the policeman's face two bullets hit him in the chest at almost point-blank range and he dropped to the grass.

The second officer quickly turned to run back to his car but two more shots rang out; one hit him in the back and the second in the head. Both men died instantly.

'Clean job. No fingerprints. No DNA and no witnesses. Now that's what I call professional.' He climbed back behind the wheel leaving the two bodies where they had dropped and making a tight circle he exited the field onto the slip road and headed on home.

No one had seen anything significant and it was more than an hour later before the bodies were discovered. There was the expected uproar in the media but in the police service there was an incredible determination to find the murderer of their colleagues. A detective chief superintendent stated on television news, 'No stone will be left unturned until the perpetrator of this crime has been brought to justice. He, or they, may hide for now, but however long it takes – we will find them.'

Needless to say, the owner of the Range Rover whose number had been checked, had a rock-solid alibi. She was a married thoracic consultant who had actually been in theatre at the time of the double murder and the CCTV at the hospital staff car park, which was timed and dated, showed her blue Range Rover to be parked there all day.

Bad Boy Buster Caulfield was too shrewd to sit back on his laurels and think the police would stop after a few cursory checks on the computer. It was time for him to take a vacation and disappear for a good spell to let the heat die down. His car, now with its legitimate number plates in place, was parked in his garage. The weapons and ammunition were taken away by a gang member. In possession of his passport, a suitcase of clothes and a large amount of cash, he was soon on a powerful RIB that very night for a scary high-speed ride across the channel. A prearranged clandestine meeting at a small French cove and Caulfield was on his way to 'Costa del Crime' in Spain, where he hoped to merge in with other criminally minded ex-pats. Sun, sea and sangria were beckoning. Life wasn't too bad really. He needed his wife to be at home so she could report any interest that might be coming their way. If things stayed quiet and there was little or no activity she could come out and join him later.

For the time-being, at least, he was a guest of

Archie Penfold, an old criminal acquaintance who had bought his retirement villa in Denia on the Costa Blanca, just north of Alicante, with the proceeds from a life of crime in the UK.

However, 'Buster' Caulfield was not quite as clever as he thought. It's true that he had been most careful to cover his tracks, but if only he had taken just a minute at the scene to look around. It would only have taken a moment to poke his head inside the police car to see the small dashboard camera looking out through the windscreen recording everything that had happened. It did not require a lot of police detection to discover what had taken place in that field. The evidence was practically handed to them on a silver platter.

Detective Inspector Adam Sinclair had nothing to do with this murder squad. It was not in his area and he was not involved in any enquiries relating to it. As a Metropolitan Police officer he was obviously affected by the shootings, like everyone else, but he was not privy to the investigation. The Caulfield address in Cobham was very soon raided and thoroughly searched. His wife, Katy, was taken in for questioning but she denied knowing anything about her husband's activities or his whereabouts and she was later released. She knew that the police would be trying to monitor calls from her mobile, she wasn't a villain's wife all these years for nothing. She contacted a girl friend of hers and borrowed her phone to make the call. Buster was shocked to hear that they were onto him so quickly. He had no idea, of course, what evidence they had but one thing he certainly did know. He had to move. If the police had learned so quickly that he was the suspect, then maybe they also knew that he was here in Spain. Although he entered France illegally, he had travelled by plane to Alicante on his British passport, just showing it for the purposes of identification at the border, but if they did a sweeping check with Europol, they might find him at some time.

Change of location without ID was needed.

On his first night with his old mate, from years back, Caulfield sat out on the patio at the rear of the property and told him the whole story.

'You've knocked the hornet's nest out of the tree this time, Buster, and they will swarm night and day to get you. They will never put this one to bed, you know that, don't you? I've never known a cop killing that hasn't ended up with an arrest.'

'Yeah, thanks for that, mate. I had no bloody choice, did I? It was them or me! With my track record I would've gone away for a long stretch,

Archie. If they had only listened to my sob story and done the decent thing they would both be alive today. I've got no sympathy for the "old bill". They got what they deserved.'

'Listen to me,' said Penfold, pouring them both another glass of scotch. 'By flying legit from France on your passport you've left a bleeding great paper trail behind you, mate. If you reckon they are on to you then it's not going to take 'em long for the "frogs" to find a record of you on a flight to Alicante, is it?'

'No choice, mate. I could get into France no problem, but I had to move quickly to Spain and didn't have the contacts to get through the border illegally. What should I do?'

'You're in luck. I've got a small, two-bed apartment not far from Sa Caleta on the south west side of Ibiza. It's not right on the coast but inland a short distance. I rent it out mostly, use it myself sometimes. There's no one in it right now. First floor with a garage underneath. I've got one of those electric, four-seat golf buggies in the garage. It's all you need to get around locally. Stay there, keep your head down and I can let you know if old bill is on the Spanish mainland sniffing around. Plug the buggy in 'cos it'll be flat, probably. You must get to Ibiza below the radar. For 200 euros I know a fishing boat that will pick you up from here, probably tomorrow night, and slip you into Sa Caleta. No conversation, no questions asked. Get a taxi to my flat and settle down. You'll be close to a few shops and a great little restaurant called "El Toro" that does the best paella in Ibiza, so they reckon. Do you like paella? I have it all the time when I go there. It's off the beaten tourist track, inland a bit, so you shouldn't get a load of nosey Brits giving you a second look. It's the best I can do for you, mate. But you must keep your head down. No fights, alright? I'll be in touch if I hear anything at all, OK?'

'Brilliant. I owe you one, Archie. Cheers mate. Do those local shops sell booze?'

And so, less than 30 hours later, the killer of two policemen had disappeared into obscurity hoping that in time the heat would die down.

The Circulation

The police, in fact, had not found Caulfield's 'footprint' in France straight away. They believed that as he must have thought he was undetected, he would be lying low in England somewhere, so they would try his old haunts before he got wind of their enquiries.

They had kept observation on his address straight away, of course, and it was only when their checks had gone cold that they brought his wife in for questioning, thus letting him know that they were on to him. It couldn't be helped.

The high-profile murder case had a detective superintendent leading the squad and he was totally committed to getting a satisfactory result before he retired.

As the initial enquiries appeared to stall, he injected new energy into the case and circulated everything about Alexander 'Buster' Caulfield on record, to all stations and all Forces, requesting any information known by any officer that may be of assistance to the enquiry. No evidence was released to the media, except that police wished to interview Caulfield regarding the murders, and his photograph was in every newspaper and on every television news broadcast.

It was then, with some nervous excitement, that Adam Sinclair, David and Jenny Sorensen got together for the first time to experiment with assisting the police in locating a known suspect. Adam wanted to be present at the experience to see first-hand how it would go. He also wanted to help Jenny with asking relevant questions as it was going to be him, after all, that would be presenting any information to the murder squad from an alleged anonymous informant.

David lay dressed comfortably in a tracksuit on top of the bed with Jenny and Adam seated in easy chairs by his side. He first studied the picture of this total stranger for some minutes and then lay back on his pillow in a drowsy state. He had insisted on doing this at 8pm because it was a sensible time with regard to any possible time zone differences.

He wanted, if possible, to view the man while he was awake and active, not while he was sleeping. Adam, of course, had no notion really of what was about to take place and watched David very closely, as this was his first time ever in this kind of experiment. He noticed nothing strange except at one point, David gave a sudden shudder or a jolt; otherwise he just appeared to be a guy dropping off to sleep.

'I am in. I am watching this man. He is in what looks like a little café or restaurant and he has just drained his beer glass. He is now paying money to a man behind the bar and is walking to the door. There is a clock above the door, and it is showing just after 9 o'clock.'

'One hour's time difference! He's in Europe somewhere,' exclaimed Adam.

Jenny frowned at him and put a finger to her lips to be quiet. David stirred and it seemed he may wake up with the loud interruption but he settled down and shortly after he spoke again. 'He has gone now. He went off down a small very dark road in an electric buggy. The sort that golfers often use. I am standing outside the restaurant which is lit up. The restaurant is called "El Toro" and a painted board outside says in English, "The finest paella in Ibiza."'

'My God! We've got him! That's all we need to know!' Adam shouted and jumped up from his chair. David also jumped and woke up. Jenny would have been angry except that Adam was so happy and jubilant she couldn't help laughing at this moment.

'Hell, David. That is unbelievable! If that's his regular diner then we've got him. At the very least we know he's in Ibiza. Have you ever been wrong on your viewing, I mean, have these guiding eyes that take you places ever made a mistake?' asked Adam.

'No. That's never happened. If you hadn't woken me up, I could have stayed with your suspect and possibly discovered his address for you. That way you could have had him locked up in Spain before daylight. Now you've got some work to do, haven't you?'

'You are dead right, of course, I'm sorry. I totally got carried away. This is so unusual and I just forgot all protocol. I apologise to you both, but hey, this is such good news! I've got to sell this now to the murder squad! El Toro restaurant in Ibiza! Wow!'

DI Sinclair was so convincing regarding the reliability of his anonymous informant, that he was seconded onto the murder squad on a temporary basis. He, and a detective sergeant, were on their way to Ibiza the following afternoon to liaise with Spanish police with a view to keeping surveillance on the 'El Toro' restaurant. Two English-speaking, uniformed Spanish police officers were allocated to Adam and his colleague and they were parked behind a disused farmhouse about half a mile away. They were armed and awaited the call by radio to 'Go, Go, Go!' from the English detectives and they would come quickly to the restaurant and all four would enter together to get the 'cop killer.' But nothing happened. Not that night. They waited from 7pm. until nearly 10:30 and there was no sign of their man. Adam and his colleague drove their hire car back to the hotel, feeling very disappointed.

'Any chance your informant got it wrong?' asked the sergeant.

Adam just shook his head, but he wondered about the possibility. They had given such a good account about this suspect and the Spanish policemen on loan to them wanted to find Caulfield almost as much as they did.

The Detective Superintendent back in the UK had organised everything so quickly he was to be admired and his enthusiasm went with the two who were now in Ibiza feeling a little bit unsure of themselves. The plan from the beginning was for the two Englishmen to meet up with their Spanish colleagues each evening until either Caulfield was arrested or the surveillance was officially called off. However, the next day, as Adam was having breakfast in the hotel restaurant, his mobile phone rang. It was the local Spanish policeman he only knew as Mateo.

'Señor Inspector, this is Mateo. Can you confirm for me that your killer may be using electricity car? Such a foreign man is now in shops here now as I am speaking. Will you come please and look? I am at the market store called "Rodeo." Your hotel is close by.'

'Keep him in view, Mateo. Stop him from leaving if he tries. I'll soon be with you.'

'Si, señor. I understand.'

When the two English officers arrived at the store, they saw Caulfield with his back against the wall with his hands on his head. Mateo was standing up close to him with his 9mm pistol rammed under his chin and staring menacingly into the villain's face.

'He did not wish to stay, señor, and he say bad words to me.'

Adam approached Caulfield and as he slipped his handcuffs onto the criminal, he informed him that he was under arrest for the murder of two police officers in England, and he cautioned him. He had never, in twenty-six years of police work, ever felt so elated at arresting someone as he did at that very moment.

'I don't have to say anything unless I wish to do so? Is that right? Good. Well I choose to say bugger all to you lot. I won't say another word.' He put on the cool, hard man act but inside he was wondering how the hell they had caught up with him so quickly. It crossed his mind that Archie Penfold may have grassed on him, maybe there was a reward he could be getting. He was the only one who knew exactly where police could find him.

It had to be Penfold, the dirty little rat. If I get life for this, I'll give everything I've got to put a contract out on him. I'll be the last person he'll ever grass up, he thought quietly to himself, as he felt the bile of hatred, violence and anger building up inside him and almost choking him.

Back in the UK Detective Inspector Adam Sinclair received a commissioner's commendation for outstanding and accurate information and the swift apprehension of a highly dangerous criminal who was wanted for the murders of two serving uniformed police officers. Alexander 'Buster' Caulfield, on the other hand, received two life sentences with no chance of parole.

CHAPTER 16

About two weeks after Caulfield's trial Jenny turned to her husband one day while they were pottering around in their garden.

'Do you realise that your last viewing with the eyes was outside the Sagittarius time zone? Did you know that? What was that about, do you think?'

'I don't know,' he replied. 'Maybe Sagittarius timing was just a red herring. Nothing to do with the eyes at all. I'm beginning to wonder if this "ability," for want of a better word, is going to stay with me the whole year round. Whatever happens, Jen, let's keep it to ourselves. There is always the danger that people could use me to a point of overload. If it transpires that I can do it all year round I think it's best that we keep that secret.'

'Absolutely. That way we are in control. If this ability became too well known you could end up being in demand all around the world. Just think of missing kids, missing people everywhere, just for a start. Then there would be a never-ending list of suspects, like Caulfield for example. It could go on and on and take over our lives.' She looked worried, but went on to say, 'Just between us, as our own little experiment, how about concentrating on a place for once, instead of a person? To see if you could view a certain area, or building or even a car for instance. What do you think?'

'Worth a try, I guess, but I don't think it will ever work backwards. I mean, I could never see what happened an hour ago or last week or last year. Nor to the future, either. It's always been at that precise moment, hasn't it?

'I've had an idea. You know my mum told us that they are having their annual dinner dance at Whitely Village? Well, it happens to be this evening. What if you just thought of the dance hall at the village before we went to bed and see if the eyes appear for a start, then secondly if they actually take you into the hall. What do you reckon?'

'OK. Let's try it this evening,' he replied with enthusiasm.

Later That Evening

It was just a casual experiment, nothing serious really. They were not actually ready for bed until 10:30pm. and David was quite relaxed about it all. As he lay back on his pillow, he allowed his thoughts to go to Whitely Village and into the entertainment hall in particular. He remembered the stage and the little office before you got into the main hall. Chairs were set around the dance floor from his memory and he was imagining several musicians playing ballroom dancing music for the residents. Then suddenly the bar of light appeared as so often before. Once again, he was in with the eyes and with a jolt, he found himself in the village hall. He was surprised that there were not that many people around. When he mumbled to that effect Jenny reminded him of the lateness of the hour and that most residents would have gone to bed by now. He noticed a lady sitting on a chair by the entrance and a man rather expertly wrapping what looked like a support bandage around her ankle.

'Which ankle, David? Left or right?'

'Left. Her shoe is off, and she is holding it on her lap. I think it's a blue strappy sandal.'

'Are musicians still around?'

'A few chaps on the stage, but the music has finished. They are packing away their instruments by the look of it. I think we are too late, but your mum is still here. She's in the hall. She is wearing a green dress and green shoes. Very smart she looks too.'

'Not too late at all, my love. I can't wait to speak to her in the morning to check out what you have just viewed. This is quite exciting. Goodnight, darling.'

David slipped into sleep.

The Next Morning

'Hello Mum? It's Jenny. Just calling to see how the dinner dance went. Was it good?'

'Oh, hello love. Yes, the band was better than last year's and the food was the usual, you know. It packed up around half ten, but I was ready for bed by then anyway. I wore that green dress I got last year for John's wedding, do you remember? Matching green shoes, everyone liked the outfit. Do you remember Myrtle Hathaway? Anyway, she used to be a professional dancer, years gone by, and was showing us some fancy dance steps she used to do, when suddenly, she slipped and twisted her ankle. A bit embarrassing for her really.'

'Oh Mum. What a shame. Which ankle was it?' Jenny asked.

'What? Oh, I don't know. What difference does it make? Left ankle I think. Yes, it was the left because I helped her back to her cottage and carried her shoe for her. That nice bar man we've got, John Pope, he's a first aider and he wrapped her foot up nicely and gave her a plastic bag full of ice to bring down the swelling when she got home.'

Jenny was smiling broadly when she came off the phone. Everything that David had viewed last night was just so accurate. When she told him about it, he was pleasantly surprised.

'Well, I still don't know how this all works,' he said. 'I wish I did. Then I could explain it to people a bit better. However, I guess this latest development, this viewing of places instead of only people, just adds another string to my bow but I'm damned if I know how it can be of any use. Do you?'

Jenny thought for a moment before shaking her head. 'No, I don't right now, but I bet we know someone who does.'

David smiled and nodded. 'Yes. Adam, of course.'

CHAPTER 17

The Boy from St. Lucia

A married couple from the West Indies island of St Lucia had been in England for almost two years with their eight-year-old son Howard. Their family name was Jeans and the boy very soon got the nickname of Blue Jeans and eventually became known at school simply as 'Bluey.'

The youngster was a naturally happy child with an irrepressible sense of fun and adventure, always looking for the next exciting thing to do. However, the sad thing about Bluey was that he had a serious renal problem which required him to attend a clinic three times a week for dialysis while he was on a waiting list for a kidney transplant.

It would be understandable for most people in such a position to feel low with this disruption to their usual, everyday routine. But not so with Bluey. He was such a jovial character who just accepted that he had a medical problem and then got on with his life, always looking for the next daring bit of fun. It was this aspect of his nature that endeared him to all who knew him.

Then one day, after school, he did not return home. As the time passed concern turned to worry, then worry turned to fear. Police were informed and, as it was disclosed that he was on such a demanding medical routine, his disappearance was treated with greater urgency. He had been to dialysis the day before, so his disappearance was not critical but very worrying, nonetheless. The boy had not done this before and could always be relied upon to come home promptly after school.

With still no sign of the boy by nightfall the incident now took on a more serious note. The following morning police had organised a television appeal to the public to look out for the missing boy and for anyone with useful information to come forward. A doctor spoke briefly about the medical urgency of finding this patient to continue the treatment and Mrs. Jeans, Bluey's mother, spoke tearfully before the cameras about her son. Her eyes, red rimmed from tears and lack of sleep, added to the grief-stricken appeal to find her baby.

Within hours a licensed taxi-cab driver had come forward to report that in the afternoon of the previous day he had witnessed something that may be helpful. In the Hammersmith area, as he stopped to pick up a fare, he noticed a man helping a young black boy into the front seat of a large white van. He did not take the number of the van, as it didn't seem suspicious at the time, but as it happened in the missing boy's area and within the relevant time zone, he thought it was worth coming forward.

The police took this latest development seriously and if nothing positive had taken place by evening they were prepared for another television appeal on the 10 o'clock news.

This time both mother and father of the boy would appear together to show solidarity and the information from the cab driver would be released, suggesting that this may have turned into a kidnapping of sorts.

The evening news appeal from Mrs. Jeans was heart wrenching. She appealed directly to her son's kidnapper to take her life instead of her boy's. She promised, before God, that she would give her life in exchange for the release of her child. It was not rehearsed nor was it practical, but it was sincere, and as the tears poured from her eyes, she clasped her hands in front of her face as if in prayer and pleaded so desperately for Bluey's life. As she and her husband sat at a long table there was an enlarged photograph of the smiling, missing boy behind them on the wall. The last few words came from a police superintendent in uniform who reminded everyone of the urgent treatment that the boy required and that without it he could only live for a short while.

Watching the news in their sitting room at home Jenny and David Sorensen were deeply touched by the sorrow of this little family. As Jenny dabbed her eyes with a tissue David reached for the TV remote control and put the news onto 'Record.'

As the programme finished, he fast reversed the recording and paused the screen with a good view of Bluey's photo on the wall. He pressed the 'mute' button on the remote, dimmed the lights in the lounge and then asked Jenny to get the voice recorder.

'We will do this one by ourselves, Jen. If anything comes of it, we can contact Adam and let him take it from there. God, I just hope the guiding eyes will come to me tonight. The timing's wrong, I know, but it may work. It did a short while back, didn't it?'

He felt quite emotional about the appeal and hoped it wouldn't jeopardise his chances of remote viewing. He settled himself back on the settee, kicked off his shoes and stared at the television image of smiling Bluey Jeans. The room in relative darkness, just a glow from the TV screen, David soon became drowsy. He continued to stare at the boy's face until eventually his eyes became too heavy and he closed them. Jenny sat at the end of the settee with her husband's head resting in her lap and cushioned on a small pillow. She held the recorder ready for action.

From the depths of his subconscious, he became aware of a piercing effulgent dot far in the distance that approached him at incredible speed. It appeared that it was travelling too fast to avoid him, but it stopped dead without slowing about one metre away from his subconscious vision. By now it looked like a narrow strip of brilliant light that quickly mellowed in its radiance until a pair of human eyes was discernible. They were the same eyes every time. David could easily recognise them by now, and he was so pleased to see them once again.

'Hello, my friend. Thank you for coming to me,' he barely whispered. The eyes slowly closed for a second or two in acknowledgement before moving very slowly forward towards him. As usual, just at the point where they would touch his face, he shuddered involuntarily and suddenly he was looking through those very eyes himself. When David was in this condition he would speak slowly with a very soft voice, but it was always clear and concise.

'The boy is here before me. He is lying in the dark and is apparently unconscious on the floor. No other person is here. It seems to me that he is injured. I can see clearly but this place is not illuminated, he is lying in the dark.'

'Is he tied up or imprisoned in this place?' Jenny quietly asked.

'This is a very old dilapidated house. It's derelict. I am looking around and there is nothing here, no furniture or anything. The place is in a filthy condition. No one lives here and there is no sign of any other person. Wait a minute. The boy appears to be in a windowless basement and looking up at the ceiling there is a big hole. It may well be that he has fallen through the ground floor rotten timbers and ended up in the cellar. I must go outside now and try to find where this place is.'

There was a long pause, then, slowly he said, 'I just cannot make out where this is. There are no other houses around, but I seem to be near a river along some footpath. I'm guessing it's the Thames but not sure. I am going back in for a moment to see if the boy has moved at all.' Jenny softly asked if there was an old number on the front door but suddenly David exclaimed, 'Oh hell! There are rats in here. Hadn't thought of that. This is becoming urgent. Jenny, the light is fading! I'm losing the eyes! Call Adam.'

Adam was with them by midnight, but David was asleep. Jenny wasn't sure what the plan was going to be but she knew this was now very serious if the boy was going to live.

'Can David wake up and just doze off again immediately to connect with the eyes?'

Jenny shook her head. 'No. We've never tried that one before. Never really needed to. It seems that after a vision he needs to rest with a proper sleep. This drains his energy somehow. It's not a simple or easy job. It takes it out of him,' she replied.

They talked and drank coffee in the lounge while David continued sleeping, until eventually they fell asleep themselves in the armchairs. At six thirty next morning David came into the room with a tray of hot tea and buttered toast and woke them up.

'Adam, thank you for coming over. I need you to be in on this right now as it has become so urgent if we are to save this lad. I've had a pretty good sleep and, although I have not tried this before, after joining you for a bit of breakfast I want to see if I can bring back the guiding eyes soon after. This is a race against the clock. There are damn rats in the building to make matters worse and the lad obviously needs his renal treatment urgently. Not to mention his concussion.'

'And dehydration!' Adam added.

'If I can even vaguely get his location will you be in a position to get a bunch of police officers to check it out?' David asked.

'Absolutely no problem. I am sure a unit of TSG would be allocated for the search after the amount of recent media cover in this enquiry.'

The Ferryman's Lodge

David's plan did work, and he successfully entered the zone again and linked-in with the guiding eyes. Adam's knowledge of London was good, which is what the Sorensens were banking on. Within two minutes of being in the zone, David identified a large commercial building across the river, almost opposite the derelict house where the young boy lay. Its trading name in large letters on the side of the building could be seen from the River Thames.

Possibly because of his recent notoriety regarding the Buster Caulfield arrest in Ibiza, the information that Detective Inspector Adam Sinclair brought to his Chief Superintendent was treated with some respect. Very soon India 99, the Metropolitan Police helicopter, was making its way along the Thames until it reached the large office building that was seen by David in his vision. Opposite that building, so the pilot reported, was an old abandoned house that was almost overgrown with foliage a short distance from the embankment. This old residence had once been the ferryman's lodge many years ago when a public commercial ferry was in operation. Within one hour, officers from the Tactical Support Group, accompanied by two paramedics, carefully entered the old house with lighting and equipment to recover the still living body of 'Bluey Jeans.'

He was in a bad way physically and they immediately put him on a drip to hydrate him before rushing him to the hospital in Charing Cross Road where he got the full range of treatment necessary to bring him back from the edge. He became the darling of the staff who nursed him back to his normal condition and, because of his sudden celebrity, photographs of the young patient in bed appeared in the media with happy reports of the missing boy's reckless act and heart-stopping rescue in the nick of time. All fears of abduction now a thing of the past.

Bluey came to accept that the stories of 'stolen gold' hidden in an old smuggler's house were probably not true after all. He also accepted that it was a very dangerous and stupid adventure in trying to find it.

The happy ending to a story that most people thought was going to end in tragedy, showed the police in a good light, and Adam's senior officers were most impressed with his unexpected input. He found the 'Jeans story' a bit difficult to pass off as reliable information from an anonymous source, as he did with Buster Caulfield. He knew that at all costs, he must keep the Sorensens out of any publicity. He had given his promise and he would stick to it – always. Over a congratulatory drink with his bosses, his chief superintendent specifically asked him how he came by such detailed and valuable information regarding the boy.

'With everyone going along with the "kidnap in a white van" theory, only you came up with the "lost boy in a derelict house" theory. Now come on, Adam, are you bloody psychic or something, eh?' his governor asked him.

Adam tried to laugh it off with the old adage, 'Well I could tell you, but then I'd have to kill you!' However, when he saw his boss's serious expression, he knew he had to come up with something more plausible. 'I knew from what I had read of the boy that he was an incurable little adventurer. I also thought that if he had in fact been kidnapped, then what the hell did the kidnappers expect to achieve? The parents have got no money and if they kept the boy for much longer, they would have a corpse on their hands as well as a murder charge in the offing. I felt it was more likely that he had gone off on some childish adventure somewhere. I know that part of the Thames fairly well from my attachment many years ago and I could remember the old ferryman's lodge as a bit of a hideout for kids from way back. It's not that far from the Jeans family flat and it just crossed my mind that the little bugger might have gone in there to explore. I took a shot at it and it paid off.'

The Chief Superintendent stared at him for several uncomfortable seconds before replying, 'That's one hell of a deduction, Sherlock. Not sure I believe it, mind you, but in the absence of anything more convincing, I'll have to go along with it I guess.'

Adam knew that to protect David's identity, he would always have to be devious about the special information that came from him. As a detective he was obviously involved almost full time with a variety of crime allegations, and it would have been so convenient to use the Sorensens to help in every case. To do that, of course, would certainly bring David to the forefront and that was to be avoided, so Adam promised to use the abilities of his friend on special cases only.

One such case came the policeman's way in late August of that year. It appeared to be a burglary, which then turned into a murder. An elderly lady, who had been a well-known face in British movies back in her day, lived alone in an expensive apartment in Kensington, London. She had done most of her work in the seventies and through the eighties and still had friends who loved her dearly, but now she lived a very quiet life and was a bit of a recluse. Her housekeeper was a younger, divorced woman called Sarah who had worked for Dame Edith for over fifteen years and often spent time with her employer even when her duties were over for the day.

The strange thing about the crime was that no one saw or heard a sound in the building, and the security camera at the entrance to the foyer revealed nothing suspicious or even unusual. The sturdy door to the apartment, although not locked from the inside, showed no signs of forced entry either.

It was Sarah's daughter, Annette, who alerted the police when she could not contact her mother, neither at home nor on her mobile phone. Knowing that her mother spent much time with the old lady, owing to their long-standing friendship, she tried contacting Dame Edith.

When even that drew a blank, Annette became worried and she, accompanied by a uniformed policeman tried without success to get a response from their knocking at the apartment door. The concierge with his pass key opened the door and all three were horrified to find a scene of bloody murder of both women.

It appeared that Sarah had put up some resistance to her attacker in the large bedroom, because things were knocked over and the room was in some disarray. She had a deep wound to the top of her head above the left eye. She also had defensive wounds to both hands and upper arms. By the look of it, she had been thrown onto the bed after the fatal blow had been administered as most of the blood was on the duvet.

The old lady had been tied to a chair in the lounge with a silk scarf and some tights from the bedroom, possibly for the purpose of interrogation before finally giving up the code number of the wall safe, as the door to it was open and the safe empty. How she died was not immediately apparent, but they felt it may well have been by heart attack from fear and old age.

The night duty CID and forensics attended and carried out all their routine work at the crime scene. Both bodies were photographed prior to removal.

The Following Day

Early next morning a murder squad was formed consisting of ten officers with Detective Superintendent Ratcliffe as senior officer in charge. Detective Inspector Adam Sinclair had been selected as his second in command. The rest of the squad consisted of two sergeants and seven detective constables. After the initial briefing they all set to work with a multitude of set tasks to do, common to all murder investigations.

By the end of day one a few important things had been learned from the initial enquiries as the squad discussed their findings in the office, prior to going home late that first night.

Neighbours, of course, were questioned but nothing very useful was gleaned except one little detail. During this particularly warm summer, it seemed that Dame Edith always left her bedroom window open. She not only wanted fresh air, but she drew comfort from the distant sound of traffic. Even in winter, apparently, her window was always slightly open. That was not really bizarre in itself, except that her apartment was the only one that always had the bedroom window open. The whole apartment had been fingerprinted, but they would have to wait a little longer for any results to come through from them.

One of the sergeants, Harry McGarry, had a theory regarding the open window. With the assistance of the concierge, he gained access to the flat roof. Bingo! Definite signs of movement on the pebbled surface just above Dame Edith's window. A one-metre-high metal rail ran all around the roof top, maybe as a safety rail or for use by window cleaners, he wasn't sure, and nor did he care. What he was sure about, was that the rail made a perfect support for a rope ladder giving access to the bedroom below.

The concierge was ruled out as a suspect. He was not a young man and besides that he needed to use a walking stick, so no acrobatic feats coming from him then. Which left Harry with the question of 'How did the burglar or burglars get onto a roof so high up?' It didn't take him long to discover that the building had a spiral fire escape at the far end which gave access to the top floor. It would need some muscular activity to get from that top platform onto the roof, but with two young men it would certainly be feasible. One could help to lift the other up and then a rope ladder could be lowered for the second to climb up after the first. For maintenance purposes, a workman would simply use a lockable hatch in the top floor corridor similar to a loft hatch, which is how Harry got up there in the first place.

'Well done, Harry,' the governor said. 'For now anyway, let's go with the theory that at least two guys entered the flat from the roof through the open bedroom window. They didn't expect to encounter a capable woman in her late forties who would put up some resistance. Maybe she started to scream. She had to be silenced quickly. Panic set in. I doubt if murder was part of the plan, but it happened anyway. What have you got for us, Tim? Anything?'

'Yes, boss. I found the old lady's solicitor from some of her correspondence and paid him a visit. She was a real character and he had met her several times over the years. It appears she had collected some "toot" in her time and probably kept it in the safe. Usual lady stuff, Couple of rings, necklace or two, brooches etc. He gave me a list of valuables that she had in her will which I've copied out for all to see. Three paintings, apart from the jewellery which were worth a fair bit and one eighteen carat gold Buddha about eight centimetres high, solid gold. Worth a lot. No sign of any of it in the flat, so I guess it's all part of the burglary.'

Adam Sinclair spoke up. 'Good job, Tim. Any chance of photographs of the jewellery and paintings for ID purposes?'

'Yes, guv. That's in hand. The solicitor will have copies for us tomorrow. He had them done for insurance purposes.'

'Excellent work. Andrea? How did you get on with the CCTV enquiries?'

'Very poor images really from the rear of the building, but two men can be seen lurking around the side alley just before nine last night. Both men were hooded up and one was carrying a large holdall. The other had a medium-sized rucksack on his back. Even when the images are enhanced you still cannot make out any detail. The camera doesn't cover the fire escape or the roof, only street level.'

Ratcliffe spoke next. 'OK Andrea, these guys have obviously done some surveillance on the place, probably in daylight. Check back a day or two on the cameras and see if anything suspicious turns up.' Andrea made a note of this in her notebook and yawned.

The SIO checked his watch and smiled.

'Not a bad start for day one. For your info there were no prints on the metal rail above the bedroom window, so we can assume they were wearing gloves. Go home, people, and rest. Be back here eight sharp tomorrow.'

Mike, the squad comedian chirped up, 'Is that

eight pm, governor?' They all laughed.

Ratcliffe smiled. 'Get the hell out of here, go on, buzz off.'

The following day there was a lull in the enquiry. Daytime cameras had picked up nothing suspicious or helpful from the previous two days. No incriminating fingerprints or DNA were found by forensics. All statements from neighbours and enquiries from residents opposite the building had drawn a blank. Mike said that he would check in with an informant of his in the underworld, in case some chatter was heard about the murders. There were still several things to do but they were routine. The first twenty-four hours of a big enquiry were the most important and usually the most productive. This had hit a plateau suddenly and the squad got on with various loose ends but nothing very significant was happening and Ratcliffe was hoping that outside information would come his way which he could expand upon. He had been on several such cases in his career, but none had fallen flat this quickly.

The photographs of the stolen property arrived on Adam Sinclair's desk, as promised, and he asked Pauline, his youngest detective constable, to get them circulated across the country in case anything was being touted for sale. As he studied the photos one, in particular, caught his eye. It was a photo of a painting signed by Pablo Picasso and underneath the picture were the words, 'From his blue period. Size 250cm x 200cm.' Adam just studied it and as he wondered how much it was worth and how difficult it may be for the killers to sell it, a sudden thought came into his head. It had been a while since the 'Bluey Jeans' case and Adam wondered if his friend David was up for helping him once again.

CHAPTER 18

'David? It's Adam on the phone. He wants to speak to us urgently. Is it OK for him to come over shortly? He can be with us in one hour,' Jenny shouted up the stairs.

'Yes, of course. I've just finished having a shower. One hour is fine, tell him.'

As Adam sat down in the Sorensens' lounge, he looked a bit apprehensive. Jenny had made them all coffee and she put biscuits out on a tray, but they were ignored.

'I know you guys haven't tried this before, well, not exactly. We've got a case that we are dealing with. It's a grizzly one, a murder most foul. No suspects, no DNA, no fingerprints and no bloody clue either. Property stolen was jewellery, a gold item and three pieces of artwork. Photos of valuables taken for insurance purposes are in our possession. One item in particular struck me. It's a small Picasso. They'll hang on to it because of its value but they might have difficulty moving it straight away, unlike the gold and jewellery. I have a good photo of the Picasso, David. What if you studied it for a while? Do you think the eyes could take you there and identify its location?'

David pondered for a minute before answering.

'I've always had success with people's faces in the past, not objects. But this is not just any old object, is it? It's a one off, unique and identifiable. I can but try, Adam. It's worth a go, eh?'

Adam looked relieved. 'You've no idea, mate. This enquiry really does need a boost, and you're the man to do it. I'm half expecting the jewellery stuff to have moved on already, which could be a problem in trying to connect it back to the murderers. If they still have the Picasso, which is likely because they will need to be very careful with it, then we could be in with a chance. I'm hoping the painting is our best bet. Are you OK to do this now? I mean it's hardly bedtime, is it?'

'It doesn't need to be. I have told you before, it's not like sleeping, it's more like being able to totally relax and slip into a dozy state. Meditation, I guess.'

'Come on then, Dozy, let's give it a try!' Adam smiled.

David was casually dressed in loose-fitting jogging bottoms and cotton T-shirt. He kicked off his slippers and sat back on the settee. 'Jen? Just pull that curtain across will you to cut a bit of the sunlight out. Thanks, hon. I am going to do this right here, in the lounge. Where's that photo of the Picasso?'

Adam passed the photo to his friend who closely studied it for a while. The detective pulled his chair up close to the settee and took a note pad and ballpoint pen from his pocket. He wanted this so much and could feel his heart racing with anticipation.

David's breathing became slower and deeper as he settled back into a relaxed state on the sofa. The house was now very quiet except for the monotonous ticking of the grandmother clock in the hallway.

Adam stared intently on his friend's face trying to interpret every nuance and expression in his bid to glean something useful out of the experience. Suddenly the breathing quickened.

'Something is wrong! I don't like this!' David's head was turning from side to side. 'Everything is pitch black and I feel closed in. Where am I? What's happening? Where are the eyes?' Jenny, as always, was close by his side to ensure his safety.

She spoke softly near his ear. 'It's OK, David. Stay calm. The eyes will come soon and there will be the usual light. Just stay with it a little longer, all right?' She sounded so confident and David nodded gently in agreement.

About two or three minutes passed and he quietly spoke again.

'I am with the eyes now. There is total darkness

here and nothing to look at. I have the usual greenish light but literally there is nothing to see. It's like being stuck in a closed box!'

It was Jenny who had the sudden brain wave first. 'David. Just move from where you are. You could be in a drawer or a cupboard. Move backwards or sideways, anyway, but just move, all right? It may well be that the picture is hidden somewhere.'

Very soon he spoke again. 'I am out of there now and in a bedroom. I was not even in a drawer but under a drawer in a bedside cabinet. The picture, I imagine, is wrapped up in something and hidden beneath the bottom drawer in this bedroom. This is very strange and a bit scary. There is a man here, he is by himself and is talking on a mobile phone. He is very angry, in a furious temper with someone and is shouting into the phone. White, but not English. Not sure where he is from, maybe Poland or Belarus. Sounds kind of Russian to me.'

Adam was so keen to make progress that he broke from protocol and spoke loudly and directly to David.

'Describe the man to me. Age, height, features, any tattoos, hair, beard, anything.'

Very quietly, his voice almost a whisper. 'Early forties. Shaved head. Not a tall man, maybe a bit under five-seven but very wiry. He is only dressed in his underwear. Strong, lean, athletic sort of look. Many tattoos, arms and chest. Slim face, clean shaven. Wild, angry eyes. I must try to find location before I lose power. Be quiet now. Don't speak.' Jenny looked at Adam and put her finger to her lips. He nodded his apology.

Agonising minutes went by and Adam wondered if David had gone off to sleep when suddenly he spoke. 'I was in a flat earlier above a tool shop. I'm now outside. This is a really busy street. The door to the upstairs flat is a dirty white PVC door to the right of the tool shop, which is called Bradley Tools. I think the power is fading.'

'Oh God, no! Jenny, please ask him, where the hell is he?'

Before Jenny could speak David continued. 'Next door to the tool shop on the left is Cricklewood Pharmacy and then a dry cleaner's shop.'

'Fan – bloody – tastic! He's on Q division! Jenny, oh Jenny, I've got to go!'

With that Adam got to his feet and swiftly departed. He made the phone call to Kilburn police from his car and David's details were confirmed one hundred per cent accurate. He now had the full postal address of the suspect's flat and was on his way to the magistrate's court to apply for a search warrant. His next call was to Superintendent Ratcliffe.

'Boss, it's Adam. I'll be with you in less than forty minutes, but I don't want to waste any time. I have new information and I'm about to get a search warrant for an address in Cricklewood as we speak. Can you get a uniform team together with a metal ram as I want to hit this drum asap before we lose any advantage?'

'What the hell has happened? What have you suddenly got that's changed anything? Last I heard we were still in the dark!'

'New info. Hot off the press. Bloody red hot an' all! See you soon and all will be revealed.' Adam was almost shaking with anticipation and adrenalin.

Later That Day

The warrant was executed, and the result was better than expected. A second man was found in the flat as armed police stormed in. Both were from Latvia and Adam had to smile to himself as he looked at one of the suspects. He was exactly as David had described him in every way. It was truly uncanny. He allowed the search to go on for a bit until he casually started checking the bedroom himself. He didn't want to make it obvious that he knew where to look but as he tipped over the bedside cabinet there, wrapped in a black cloth, was Dame Edith's Picasso. As he carefully placed it into an evidence bag, he said, 'I'll wager I know whose prints are going to be found on this little beauty.' Two items of jewellery from the murder were found in the second man's jacket. Apparently when trying to sell them he felt he was being offered less than what they were truly worth and came away without a deal. Hence the blazing argument that David had witnessed, but of course that would always remain a secret between him and the Sorensens. The murder weapon was never found but the finely made nylon and steel wire ladder was rolled up into a tight tubular shape and was found stuffed in a backpack under one of the beds, kept probably for future jobs.

It was a very praiseworthy result for the squad and Adam was given full recognition for its success. Martin Ratcliffe, if anything, was sorely envious of his second in command but was genuinely delighted to have had him on the team. And so he should have been! If not for Adam and his amazing informant there would have been no chance of solving that gruesome crime in such swift order.

Adam kept the Sorensens posted of the arrests and

was most grateful for their assistance. When the case finally came to court both men were found guilty of the robbery and the murders. Life sentences were given to both men and once again a commendation went to Detective Inspector A. Sinclair, and on that high, Adam prepared to retire from the Metropolitan Police having completed thirty years of good and interesting service. However, before that would take place there was to be one last investigation for him to deal with, and it would have to involve the help of David Sorensen.

CHAPTER 19

Danny Mulcahy had crossed the water by ferry to Liverpool and had boarded the train to London. He sat by the window and gazed at England for the first time as the train raced its way south. His face showed no expression but he felt the excitement coursing through his body and he let his mind wander back over the years to the days of his youth.

He was the eldest of five children born to Catholics, Annie and Billy Mulcahy in South Armagh. The whole area was very Republican and although not much was ever said to him it was obvious to the boy that his Da was involved with the IRA.

Billy would often take his eldest son hunting at the weekend, shooting for rabbits, pheasants and if they were lucky, a deer for the freezer. The boy knew from an early age that his Da was an excellent shot with the rifle and rarely did he ever miss what he was aiming for. Over the years Danny was encouraged to use a lighter rifle than his father's and with his Da's coaching, he also became a crack shot. At these times, when the two of them were alone, Danny would quiz his Da about the whole political scene in Ireland and learned from the one man he most loved, respected and admired, how life really was in their beloved Ireland and how the United Kingdom had been conquerors in their country for too long. Talking would never get through to the government in Westminster, to give Ireland total independence; only through aggression would they see that Irish men were serious and would never give in to the force of bullying.

'Erin go Bragh, my lad. Erin go Bragh! Do you know what that means?' he once asked Danny.

'Not too sure, Da,' he replied.

'Ireland till the end of time! That's what it means. Ireland till the end of time. Don't you forget that, Danny, my boy. Long after we are both gone, this beautiful land of ours will still be here and what we do today, our fight for independence, will give the kinfolk of tomorrow a country to be proud of. Not some crushed and conquered nation, divided and occupied by unwelcome foreigners!'

He could hear the emotion in his father's voice, and he knew then that his Da was a real fighter for freedom. The pride swelled up in the young heart of Danny Mulcahy, the pride of being his father's son.

South Armagh was not called bandit country for no good reason. From 1991 the IRA waged a fierce war against the military forces and the RUC. Army patrols were ambushed and South Armagh in particular, had an Active Service Unit, or ASU, that prided itself on its effective sniper squads which played havoc with police patrols and the low-flying military helicopters. Billy Mulcahy was probably the best sniper in the ASU and was responsible for downing two helicopters and killing many soldiers and police constables. The IRA in that region felt invincible, so in 1994 when there was an agreed ceasefire from both sides for the purpose of peace talks, the South Armagh Brigade of the IRA decided to ignore it and carry on with their actions. Their commanders felt it displayed weakness as well as giving the enemy an opportunity to build up their list of informants. They believed that the war should continue despite what other Provo units did and Billy Mulcahy was in full agreement. One day in 1995, almost one year after the official ceasefire was declared, Billy was spotted by an Army patrol as he hid in some undergrowth waiting to attack them. A short fire fight took place and Billy was shot dead.

His funeral was a grand affair with so many supporters and friends attending as well as receiving the illegal IRA armed salute by masked ASU gunmen. Before the service began his open casket was placed in the church for people to pay their last respects. Danny was seventeen two days prior to the funeral and he stood by the casket with tears in his eyes.

As the church began to fill up, he noticed three men approaching him. They were the hard men of the Brigade and he had seen them before with his da. Gerard McGuigan, Declan Maloney and Ruairi O'Connor, each one shook Danny's hand and kissed him on both cheeks.

'He was my hero. He was me Da and me hero,' he cried as the men stood around him.

McGuigan placed an arm across his shoulders and said to him, 'Danny, let me tell you this in all truth. Your Da was the best there is and no mistake. He will be greatly missed, not only by you and the rest of the family, not just by the Brigade but by the whole Republican movement. He was a champion among us and you should be so proud.'

The wake was held in the church hall with much food and drink laid on by friends and supporters and Danny had taken advantage of a couple of glasses of Irish whisky.

At one point, Ruairi O'Connor sauntered over to him and sat the lad down in a quiet corner. 'They say you're a chip off the old block, Danny. Is it true what they say?'

'What do you mean, sir? I'm like me Da do you mean?'

'I mean you're a feckin' good shot with a rifle like your old man was. Is it true?'

Danny felt embarrassed but nodded with a smile.

'Don't be shy, lad, be proud of what Billy taught you. Those foreign soldiers took your dad's life in his own country when they had no right to even be here. That is a wickedness that I for one can never forgive. Can you?'

'No, sir.'

'I'm not a sir, Danny. I'm Ruairi. The scales are way out of balance, my boy. Your Da was worth God knows how many of them and that needs to be readdressed. Can you see yourself avenging Billy's death with our help and guidance?'

'Yes, I can, Ruairi. It is my duty as his eldest son.' With that Danny picked up his whisky glass and held it high above his head then shouted loudly, 'Erin go Bragh.'

Many in the hall turned to look at him before shouting their reply, 'Erin go Bragh!'

The ceasefire lasted until 1996 but then the violence started all over again involving all the IRA, by which time Danny was his father's son in more ways than one. By then he was confirmed in the league of Republican killers.

CHAPTER 20

As the train pulled into a station the screeching of brakes suddenly woke him from his reverie. That was fifteen years ago, he realised. He was now thirty-two and so much had happened since those early days. He looked around the compartment at the other travellers and smiled inwardly to himself. If only they knew what he was going to do in their country, they would be horrified. If only they knew that they had been sitting near the man who would be responsible for the headlines of their daily newspapers for days to come!

Let them have a taste of what it's like to have an enemy on their home soil bringing death and havoc to their orderly system of life, he mused.

He hadn't needed a passport to make the journey. Only photo ID was required and the driving licence in his wallet with his photo on it in the name of Patrick Kirlin looked authentic enough, which of course, it wasn't. He opened his backpack to check, once again, the envelope with a front door key in it. He had memorised the address of the little rented London flat that had been organised by O'Connor and paid for some weeks earlier. Danny carried no weapon, not even a penknife. His fingerprints were unknown, and he was untraceable. He was what they called 'a clean skin.' On his arrival at the rented flat he would find the weapon and ammo in its case under the bed. If he successfully carried out this attack it would be an even greater, more devastating blow to the British establishment than the assassination of Lord Louis Mountbatten back in '79 off the coast of Mullaghmore. Yes, everyone knows about the Good Friday Agreement of 1998, but it wasn't an agreement made by Danny Mulcahy or his close-knit band of boys from South Armagh. They ignored it.

When he got to Euston station, he quickly found a London black cab and gave the driver the address and post code of the flat from memory. The building was old, and the flat was at the top on the third floor. He knocked on the door as a precaution and when there was no reply, he quietly let himself in. Almost immediately he checked under the bed and found the large plastic box which he opened while sitting on the bed. As expected, he found inside the Barret M82 sniper rifle, scope and box of 50 calibre rounds. This was a cannon of a rifle and had been in London for a while, reserved for just this occasion. Opposite the flats, across the road, was an Esso garage which was brightly lit and as darkness fell Danny had a good view onto the street below while his front bedroom light was turned off. He took the rifle box into the kitchen at the back and spent over thirty minutes stripping the weapon down, cleaning it and reassembling it.

Although he was hungry, he was also very tired, and as it was still early evening, he decided to grab some rest before going out to find a pizza bar or fish shop. Taking out his burner phone he set the time alarm for eight o'clock and placed it on the bedside cabinet. He then kicked off his shoes and lay on the bed. Within two minutes he was asleep.

Somewhere in the darkness he was dreaming. He was with his Da sitting around an outside fire cooking meat on sticks. He could smell the fire and the smoke, but now the smoke was making him cough and he woke up. As he looked around he could see smoke filling the room. Jumping off the bed he raced into the narrow hallway and immediately noticed thick smoke pouring under the door to the flat and he knew he had to get out quickly. He ran back into the bedroom, slipped his shoes on and grabbing his backpack in one hand he gripped the handle of the rifle box with the other. The hallway was now so smoky he could hardly see, but he swiftly made his way to the door and, dropping his backpack he pulled it open.

Almost immediately, as he was looking downwards, he saw the cause of the smoke. Four smoke pellets had been lit and wedged under the door. They were the sort of smoke pellets that are used against wasp nests and checking the updraft of open fires. It took hardly a second for this to register but as he raised his head, he saw a man standing very still on the landing about a metre away and his arm was straight and pointing at Danny's head.

There was no time to speak or to react in any way before two muffled thuds sounded and Danny was hurled backwards. He was dead before he hit the floor. The man took a small tin box from his jacket pocket and using the lid he scooped the remains of the smoking pellets back into the box and closed the tightly fitting lid back in place and the smoke ceased. He then slipped on a pair of surgical rubber gloves and entered the flat, leaving the dead body where it lay, just pulling the feet away in order to shut the door. Leaving the lights off he made his way into the bedroom and opened a window to clear the smoke. Carrying the rifle container into the kitchen he turned those lights on and took the heavy weapon out to check it and photograph it on his mobile phone. He next went back into the hall and took a photo of Danny's face before slipping his phone back into his pocket.

Suddenly the burner phone started peeping in the bedroom. He went in and turned the alarm off but immediately dialled 999 and asked for the police. When he got through to New Scotland Yard his message was very brief. In a soft, disguised voice he gave the control room the address he was at and told them there was a dead body in the hall. He ended the call before they could ask any questions. Leaving the rifle where it was on the kitchen table he dropped the burner phone onto the dead man's body, swiftly left the building and was swallowed up by the night.

The Final Case

'C'mon, Adam. I want you on this squad. Don't give me all that retirement bull. I know you and I need your expertise. It's a tricky murder case and you'll love trying to undo the knots. I've got Tommy Lovelock on the team as well and you two are mates, aren't you?'

Adam thought for a moment before replying. 'Are you SIO on this one, Derek, or are they bringing in the brass?' He was talking to Detective Chief Inspector Potter, a friend he had known and worked with on many cases in the past.

'Just me, mate. What do you say? Give it your best shot?'

'Can we crack it in seven weeks? 'Cos that's all the time I've got left in the job. It's a "booked and paid for" holiday after that. Can't miss that one, can I?'

'Of course we can! With you, me and Tommy in the team it will be like old times. Briefing at my nick, nine tomorrow morning. They've given me the new annexe for this job so we will have plenty of room. Call this one your Swan Song, Adam. Go out with a bang, eh? The rest of the squad are handpicked too. We've got some experience working with us. See you tomorrow, bye for now.'

CHAPTER 21

Detective Chief Inspector Derek Potter introduced himself to the newly formed squad, for those who didn't already know him, and immediately went into the peculiar circumstances of the case.

'Victim is a white male around thirty years or so with no apparent previous convictions. Only ID is a driving licence from Northern Ireland which uniform are already checking out for us. Shot twice at close range in a rented flat on our manor. Now here come the odd bits. It appears the killer used the victim's burner phone to call the Yard and report the murder. When uniform got there, the phone was lying on the dead man's chest and in the kitchen was the biggest bloody rifle you've ever seen, complete with scope, box of huge calibre bullets, tripod and cleaning kit. We are talking assassination kit here, ladies and gentlemen, and the killer left it for us to find. Very kind of him. Must say, "Thank you," when we nick him.'

The members of the squad were duly given their initial routine tasks to begin with, all the basic stuff had to be checked and looked at and everyone was keen to get a result on this strange murder case.

When it transpired that the victim's ID was false, that threw a spanner in the works, for the squad had no relatives to question, no acquaintances, no hometown or anything to suggest who he was. This made it a little tricky trying to find out who would want to kill him. The rifle didn't help much either. Apart from sharp intakes of breath and words of admiration from the firearms department, not much more could be gleaned.

After a couple of weeks DCI Potter called his two DIs into his office. 'Listen, gents, let's talk this through together. We've got an obvious assassin who hasn't done the job yet, box of bullets complete and gun not fired. Along comes our killer, takes out the assassin very expertly with two .38 bullets, one through the heart and one through the throat. No resident witnesses and no one in the building heard a shot. Sounds like our killer may have used a silenced gun, which leads me to consider that he also is a professional shooter. Are we in agreement so far?'

Tommy Lovejoy nodded approval and added, 'I know his ID is false, but he could well be Irish anyway, so I've sent a photo of his face to the RUC in case any of them can recognise him. The lack of passport and only a dodgy driving licence suggests to me that he was either going to hire a car and wanted anonymity, or that he really came from Ireland and that's the only ID he needed. Anyway, I'm checking Liverpool to see if and when he came to England, as well as the airports. It won't tell us who he is but it may tell us how long he's been here.'

'Good one, Tommy. Keep me posted on that. Adam? Anything?'

'Yes. CCTV very thin on the ground in that area, but there's an Esso garage opposite the Crime scene and their cameras run 24/7. The place is run by Asians and they haven't really been helpful but I've tracked down the senior management and they are very cooperative. I should have the discs by this afternoon. It's always worth a try.'

'Good work,' said the boss, then added, 'Talking of CCTV, the killer either came to the flat either by car or on foot. Have you checked further afield to get a possible suspect?'

'Apart from the garage everything around there is old residential property and cameras are either dummies or just not fitted. I drew a blank on that one. Our only hope is the garage, but I'm not sure if their cameras pick up stuff across the road. I should know soon enough.'

By late afternoon, as promised, Adam had the disc

for the late shift on the day of the murder. It was a safe bet that the killing took place at the time of the phone call to the Yard, so he looked in slow motion for half an hour before and after eight pm. The cameras did view across the road, in case of drive-outs without payment etc. and the images, especially of people at night, were not very good. There was nothing to see before eight o'clock owing to a spate of lorries and buses going past but shortly after eight there was a brief lull in road activity and a man could be seen coming out of the main doors leading to the flats. Adam obtained a still photo from the video which made the image very grainy, but one could still make out the man's clean-shaven features. There was nothing unusual about his build or his clothing – tight jeans, trainers and what looked like a black bomber jacket on top of a dark shirt or sweater. Adam stared hard at the face under a microscope but that didn't make the features any clearer. He sent it to the police laboratory to see if they could enhance the photo but even after their attempts to lighten the background and enlarge the image it didn't help much with the clarity. Then a great idea struck him.

'Hi David, it's Adam. Guess what? I've got an unusual one for you. It really is different. Can I come over?'

The investigation suddenly now involved David Sorensen!

It was late when Adam came over and he, David and Jenny sat in the kitchen and the two men shared a pizza while Jenny listened intently to the grizzly story that Adam poured out. Strictly he should not have divulged confidential details of an on-going investigation to an outsider, but he could never regard the Sorensens as outsiders, especially when they were helping with a murder investigation.

'Adam, I wish to do this one tomorrow with just Jenny and me. I want to do it in the daytime so if it works, I will hopefully see this guy when he is awake, and maybe see where he is. I have your mobile number and if anything useful crops up I will be onto you straight away. Is that OK?'

David left them with three versions of the same photo, a postcard-sized original, an enhanced one with a lighter background and an original like the first only A4 size. By late morning of the following day David and Jenny had successfully completed the experiment with the 'Eyes' and Jenny, as usual, had made a typed transcript on 'Word' from the recording of David's remote viewing experience.

'Hi Adam. Can you speak? I have something positive to tell you.'

'No. Too many people around. I'll find a quiet spot and call you back. Give me five minutes, David, is that OK?'

'Sure. I'm not going anywhere. Speak soon. This will amaze you.'

A few minutes later the two friends were talking. David did not want to read the whole transcript to Adam over the phone, so he went directly to the main gist of what he saw. 'I found your man. He was in a small room packing clothes into a suitcase. On the bed, a single bed, were some scattered papers and a red folder. Written in bold letters on the folder was the following; Sgt. R.L. Manfield and one of the sheets of paper had writing in ink that started, "Dear Richard," I assumed the guy was a policeman or a soldier with the "Sgt." abbreviation for sergeant so I went with the eyes out of the building towards the exit where I saw a large sign that read, "22 Special Air Service Regiment." Adam, your man is SAS from Hereford! What will you do?'

There was a lengthy silence.

'Adam? Are you there? What will you do?'

'David, are you absolutely sure the guy you saw, this Sergeant Manfield, was the same guy in the photo?'

'Without a doubt, my friend. The eyes have never let me down and his live features were clearly those of the chap in the photo. In addition, he was wearing a thin, black polo neck sweater beneath a black leather bomber jacket. Good luck, Adam, in whatever you do.'

'How the hell am I going to present this to Derek Potter and the rest of the squad? This is a stinker for sure! I may have to follow this line of enquiry off the record by myself. I could never bluff a story to the squad that I just happened to think our killer is a guy in the SAS. It might as well be the bloody man in the moon! Thanks, David. Leave this with me for now. I've got some serious thinking to do.'

For the rest of the day Adam agonised over his dilemma and finally decided to make an enquiry of his own initiative. If it became official then he would have some very tough explaining to do, but right now, he couldn't simply forget what he had learned. As they say, he was somewhere between a rock and a hard place.

The next morning, he tried to telephone the commanding officer of the SAS and have an 'Off the record' chat with him, if it's ever possible for a detective to speak off the record about a murderer that he's trying to trace. He got through all right but had to leave messages twice for a return call.

Finally, Adam received his call and was surprised to find he was a charming, although 'No Nonsense' kind of man. Adam's initial approach was to ask if it was possible to speak to Sergeant Richard Manfield regarding a police matter. He was politely but firmly told, 'No. Our position is that we do not divulge the names of our members, so I can neither confirm nor deny if we even have a soldier by that name. If, however, you needed to interview one of my men you would need to be much more forthcoming with your details. For example, what's this all about?'

Adam's next approach was to release more information and merely suggest that Manfield may have information that could assist police in a murder enquiry.

'How do you think a soldier of mine could assist in a murder enquiry? Do you mean as a suspect?'

He took the bull by the horns. 'It's just that Sgt. Manfield was pictured on a CCTV camera around the time and location of a murder a couple of weeks ago and I wondered if he had seen anything at that time that might help us with our enquiries. It would be so useful if he had.'

'Sgt. Manfield, you say? You talk as if you know him. Are you positive there is a soldier from this regiment by that name?'

'Yes, sir. Positive,' he lied. 'However, there is no question of making any allegations right now. We are still searching for evidence and information. That's where we are at the moment, so any help that he could give us would be most appreciated.'

There followed several seconds of silence.

'Detective Inspector Adam Sinclair, you say? Right. I've made a note of your contact details and I'll tell you what I'll do. I'll do some checking of my own, see if we even have such a soldier in the regiment, and I'll also see if there's anything that he may know to help you. Give me a wee while. I will get back to you. Goodbye.'

Adam felt some apprehension and wondered how this was all going to pan out. The CO was undoubtedly cautious, of course he would have known if someone by that name and rank was in the regiment. He was obviously playing for time, Adam concluded, but the ball was now in the Army's court.

Just as Adam was about to get some lunch the following day his phone rang and a rather cultured voice introduced himself as the 'serving under-secretary of state to the Home Office.'

'I am making this call as a direct request of the Home Secretary. I must make it clear that this is not an order from government but an unofficial advisory conversation. The fact is that the Commanding Officer of the SAS has held a video conference with the Home Secretary with regards to your enquiries into a recent fatal event in London. Now, in case you were unaware, SAS soldiers are occasionally called upon to carry out highly confidential, and often top-secret missions, in order to protect our society and the rule of law and order. Without alluding to any particular event or venue I can confirm that just recently there came to light a plan of immense gravity upon mainland Britain, and had it succeeded the repercussions would have been devastating for British morale and would have rocked the foundations of our society for many years to come. It may be that whatever your enquiries are, they could inadvertently be picking away at the edges of a mission that was sanctioned to protect us and our way of life. It comes under the banner of National Security. Is this beginning to make any sense to you, Inspector?'

Adam stood his ground. 'Sanctioned? Are you suggesting, sir, that a would-be assassin was murdered by government decree?'

In the silence that followed Adam clearly heard a deep sigh over the phone.

'I see you are a man who prefers naked brevity to a comprehensive explanation of the facts. I will say this to you and no more. If you feel that it is impossible to withdraw from your line of enquiry, then kindly let me know for sure within the next twenty-four hours, for after that it will be out of my hands.'

Adam was quick to reply. 'What does that mean exactly? What happens if that does occur?'

'Then the Home Secretary will request a meeting with the Commissioner of the Metropolitan Police and explain the protocol of the Official Secrets Act of 1989, in particular the passage relating to the security and defence of the realm. Also, as a matter of security, Inspector, he will ask the Commissioner how it was possible that you decided that the full name, rank and occupation of an undercover operative in Her Majesty's armed forces applied to a distorted image, at best, of a photograph taken from a CCTV video at night-time. A most interesting jump to conclusion which, should this become an official enquiry by the Home Secretary, you would be only too pleased, I'm sure, Inspector, to explain your findings in great detail. I expect to hear about your decision within the next twenty-four hours.'

The line went dead and left Adam staring blankly into an empty coffee cup on his desk. He sat thinking quietly to himself for some time. *Oh, David. This is getting too hot, my friend. Too damned hot. It's time to back out before it gets any hotter.*

He knew only too well that if this went much further, then he would certainly be required to explain where this information came from and how it was that the assassin was traced to the SAS barracks in Hereford.

CHAPTER 22

D CI Potter met him in the corridor. 'Hi, Adam. I meant to catch up with you. Any result on the garage CCTV? I heard that you sent something off to the lab for enhancement?'

'It was useless, Derek. Just a grainy shot of some bloke on the pavement, so distorted it could have been anyone really. I don't think we can get any further with that one.'

The enquiries continued until they ran out of steam and most of the squad were disbanded.

Adam's retirement arrived at last then he and Gillian went on that holiday to Canada's Rocky Mountains. On his return he called round to see his old friends, the Sorensens, at their Twickenham address and insisted on making a date to take them out, just the four of them, for a dinner.

Some days later he and Gillian picked them up by chauffeured limousine and took them to a Michelin star restaurant for what was probably the best food any of them had ever consumed.

He was very fond of David and Jenny and so grateful for the help they had given him with his police work. 'I've got to know you both so well over the years and greatly admire the pair of you. I always kept you concealed from any publicity, like I promised, not even telling my close friends about you. I didn't even invite you to my retirement bash in case enquiring eyes and nosey parkers started asking who you were.'

'Thank you, Adam. Jenny and I have always felt safe working with you and it's been so fulfilling knowing we could help in some way.'

When the two wives went off to the rest room together Adam leaned forward and spoke softly.

'How is it that you can just drop off to sleep at any time, David? It always takes me ages, and secondly, can you "tune in" to anyone and secretly see what they are up to at that very moment? That could turn out to be a bit embarrassing at certain times, couldn't it?'

'When I have an experience with "the eyes," it seems to tax my energy somehow and I just sleep. Most nights are just normal for me and I only have the guiding eyes experience when I really want to. Normally, like you it can take a while to drop off, especially if I'm thinking about problems or personal matters, just like anyone else, I guess. As for your second question, the answer is no. I am not some kind of seedy voyeur, Adam. I only ever study a person if it has some important significance or principle behind it. I never study anyone just for the hell of it.'

Adam smiled and drained his wine glass. 'You are probably the most principled man I've ever met, David. I really mean that.'

Back at Twickenham, having just dropped off his two guests, Adam shook David's hand warmly and hugged Jenny closely. 'Look, this does not mean an end to us, OK? I may not be a copper anymore, but you're our dear friends and I don't want to lose touch with you. Do you hear me? Let's make a promise right here and now, a round of golf once a month, OK, then evening dinner just the four of us. What do you reckon?'

They laughed and readily agreed. David and Jenny stood side by side and waved Adam and his wife goodbye, as the hired limousine drove off. David stood by his gate looking down the road as the rear lights faded, until they finally disappeared. He was smiling broadly, slightly drunk from the fine wine they had consumed at the restaurant. Little did any of them know that this night would be the last time he would ever see Adam. Right now, he felt very fortunate to have found such a good friend who not only understood and accepted his strange ability, but he was someone he could trust and confide in.

CHAPTER 23

'Hi. My name is Frank Bulducci, from the American embassy. Could I speak to Mr. David Sorensen please?' For a moment David paused as he heard the American accent and wondered what would come next.

'Yes, that's me. Can I help you?' David's soft voice sounded formal and he beckoned to Jenny across the room to approach the telephone so she could hear the call.

'Mr. Sorensen, I flew in from the USA last night specially to see you and I wondered if you could spare me a little time to speak with you. It is kind of urgent. I am with the Agency and I do have official sanction to be here. Before saying another word, can I suggest that you phone back here, to the US embassy in London, to verify my name and status? Do you have their number?'

'Yes, I do. But who is Frank Bulducci and what exactly do you want?' David replied.

'Make the call, Mr. Sorensen. Crozier is not here, of course. Not after all this time, and nor is Ruben Dexter but if you ask the reception for security, they will connect you to the chief man called Stapleton. I'll speak to you soon.' The phone clicked off, leaving

David and Jenny staring at each other.

The embassy switchboard transferred David's call to security and a man called Stapleton confirmed that Bulducci was, indeed, a special agent from the CIA and transferred the call to another office which Bulducci was temporarily occupying.

'I'm sorry to tell you that JD Casey sadly passed away a few weeks ago and some of his more sensitive files were transferred from the Bureau to the Agency. It was from one of them that I learned about you, Mr. Sorensen. Does operation 'Eagle Eye' ring a bell?'

The man spoke quickly as if in some sort of a hurry. David was surprised by this news and thought back with mixed feelings to the days when he worked with the FBI man.

'Sorry to hear about Mr. Casey,' David answered. 'How did he die?'

'Usual thing in our line of work. Sudden heart attack. Didn't actually know the guy personally but I hear he was good at what he did. I don't like business over the phone, Mr. Sorensen. Hey! Can I call you David? Feel free to call me Frank. Anyway, phone lines are not secure. You at home tomorrow? What if I come to you, say around 10am? Will that be OK? Need to talk, shouldn't take long. What do you say?'

Jenny could hear clearly as David had put the call

on 'speaker' and as he looked at her with raised eyebrows, she nodded approval.

'Yes, that would be convenient. Ten o'clock tomorrow then. Goodbye.'

The Offer

Bulducci was a thickset man with dark cropped hair and penetrating eyes and Jenny didn't like him. He was very serious and hard looking, and she felt slightly scared of him. David held his judgement until he got to know the man better. He refused any offer of refreshment and was looking at his watch even before he sat down in the armchair.

'I will be quick and to the point. I have read Casey's file on your work with him and I know everything that happened and everything there is about the two of you, so there's no need for long explanations or the like. Why Casey did not use you for the obvious cause of locating Bin Laden I will never know. It may be that back then we really thought he was in the Tora Bora mountains which he knew all about from his days fighting the Soviets. One thing I do know and it's this. We don't have a clue where this bastard is now hiding.

'Our new president is committed to finding Bin Laden and he has put great trust in the CIA to catch him. Originally there were about three or four different departments involved with the search, FBI being just one of them, but as the years have gone by it appears that it's mainly down to us now in the Agency. I work quickly and my input into everything I do is intense. I have powerful backing and a big wallet and I expect results. You would be working for me only and I expect that your efforts should not be required for long. Days, not weeks. Your flight to the States and your return is in business class, your secure accommodation is supplied by us and you will have $400 a day expenses as a couple. Need I remind you that if your information, your specialist ability, is responsible for locating the whereabouts of OBL and his subsequent capture or death, you would qualify for the reward of $25 million. How soon can you both be ready to leave?' He looked at his watch once again.

'In case you weren't aware, my last efforts to assist, got me blown up and severely injured, after your government felt obliged to freeze my capital for one year to keep me in America, when all I wanted to do was to come home!' David replied curtly. 'Take nothing for granted, Mr. Bulducci. You'll get no snap decision from us today, but we will talk this over and let you know as soon as we have made up our minds, one way or the other.'

His eyes bore into David as he sat back in the armchair and crossed his legs.

'I know all about the assassination attempt. That was down to Songbird singing too loudly and she put herself and you in grave danger. For that she met a violent death, so her sudden wealth did her no good at all. But it did pay for a lavish funeral.'

David was shocked. 'Who killed her? This Songbird, I mean?'

The American frowned. 'Are you thinking we did it? Not at all! Most likely the same people who were after you. Jihadist sleepers. Let me assure you, I will guarantee your security if you come over the pond, and that's a promise. You will have one or two agents shadowing you wherever you go, providing you cooperate with them and let them know when and where you are going beforehand. No harm will come to either of you in the States. Not on my watch.' He sounded genuine and, as he rose to his feet, he checked the time again.

'I look forward to your call. Please treat this as urgent, OK?' He shook hands briefly with David and nodded to Jenny. 'Pleasure to meet you, ma'am.' Just as quickly, he was gone.

The Acceptance

It was a foregone conclusion really that the Sorensens would accept the American's offer.

David knew that as long as this ability continued with him, he felt some obligation to put it to good use. This latest offer was probably the most momentous task that they were ever likely to undertake. At this moment in world news, the capture of Osama bin Laden would be a leading story in every country and a huge smack in the face for global terrorism. It would show that no matter who you were, or how big you think you might be, if you represent terror, then you cannot hide from justice forever. Sooner or later justice will find you and come knocking on your door.

'Mr. Bulducci? Hello, it's David Sorensen.' David called back as requested late the next morning. 'Jenny and I have discussed your offer very carefully and I am pleased to say that we accept it. I would like to make two points before we go any further. Firstly, I want your absolute promise to ensure our safety and anonymity. I am only too aware that there are people who got to know who I am and what I could do to upset their plans and their cause, and those people were in the USA. "Sleepers," I think JD called them.'

'You have my total guarantee that as long as you are on American soil you will be covered by CIA security. Of course, I cannot guarantee anything in Britain, but I guess you've got that covered already, haven't you?' Bulducci asked. David hadn't, but it certainly was food for thought. There was no immediate reply so the American continued.

'You said two points. What's the second?'

'Oh yes. It's about the reward money. If we have success in this venture, and I feel we have a very good chance of that, I want it on record that we are not interested in the reward money. We neither need it nor want it. We now have wealth which is more than sufficient for the rest of our lives. We will try to help but it is not for the money, OK? You can ask Mr. Barrack Obama to use it on something really worthwhile. Also, it would be nice to know that if we wish to stay for a while in America and plan a grand tour, we won't encounter visa problems or the like? Could that be arranged?'

Bulducci smiled to himself and made a note on the pad in front of him.

'Shouldn't be a problem,' he said. 'I'm surprised what you said about the money. Never known anyone to say no to twenty-five million greenbacks. Maybe that's what makes you Brits kind of unique. Can you make a morning flight day after tomorrow?'

David thought for a while and was looking at his wife who could hear the conversation.

'Yes, OK. We have some things to arrange here before we go. There's Jenny's mother to notify and say goodbye to. We have a good friend who will check on the house while we're away, things like that. Yes, day after tomorrow will be fine.'

'You will get a call from the embassy tomorrow some time. If you're not in it can go on your answer phone. It will be the details and time of flight etc. for the following day. I'm glad you made the right decision, feller, and I look forward to working with you. Goodbye.'

As the phone went dead David thought, *If he cannot call me Mr. Sorensen and starts with the 'feller' routine then I must insist on being called David. Oh God! He'll then tell me to call him Frank!*

CHAPTER 24

Back in the USA

Their arrival at CIA HQ at Langley was a bit of an experience for them both but everything had run smoothly and had been uneventful. Just like it was years ago with the FBI, they were not really introduced to anyone other than the main person handling them.

Bulducci was there of course, as he had returned the previous day. They sat in his office while he looked through a slim plastic briefcase, checking its contents carefully. Finally, he appeared satisfied and pushed it across his desk towards them.

'OK, feller, it's all there. Two mobiles strictly for business. Paperwork you will need to enter and exit the building. Two cash cards for your use while you are here, there's four hundred on the account right now and each midnight it gets topped up with another four hundred. There's a card with telephone numbers on it that you may need, mainly me and your contact shadow agents. It's Saturday now. Let's take tomorrow off. Get over the journey and all, go see the sights if you like, but be back here at eight-thirty Monday morning. You will get a lift to your safe house now and will be picked up at seven-thirty sharp, on Monday. Don't forget, any problems, any plans, let your shadows know, OK? Got any questions?'

'Yes, just one,' said David. 'Can you please not call me "feller"? I would prefer it if you called me David.'

Bulducci stared at him for several seconds and then broke into a wide grin and his eyes softened. Jenny thought he almost looked quite normal and not so scary when he did that. Maybe he should do it more often.

'Sure. Not a problem, Dave. Call me Frankie. Enough of this "Mr. Bulducci" crap.'

The agent who drove them from the airport was available to drive them and their luggage on to their safe house. His name was Randy, but he was not one of the two guys allocated to be their shadows. Their names and mobile numbers were on the card in the briefcase. Randy was a friendly chap and chatted away quite amiably as they made their forty-minute journey from the HQ.

'Tell me something, Randy,' Jenny asked. 'We are off tomorrow. Any suggestions as to what we can see or visit, that's not too far away? It can only be a cab ride, so somewhere local I think.'

'Hell yes. Try the Smithsonian Institution. It's a

huge complex with loads of things to see. For me, the best is NASM, that's the National Air and Space Museum. It's the most visited museum in the whole country and it's fabulous! It has the largest and most comprehensive collection of artefacts in the history of human flight. One of the best bits for me was the space shuttle and module and those virtual reality "gizmos," hell, it's just the real deal. And it's for every age. I'm sure you'll love it. Just ask the cabby for the NASM.'

'That sounds very interesting, Randy. Thank you. We might well give that a visit,' Jenny said.

'Two things to consider,' chipped in Randy. 'Go as early as you can to beat the tourists 'cos it does get real busy. Secondly, those cards you were given are cash cards. Just go to an ATM and get some cash. Cabbies prefer that and cash is good for a coffee or a dog, OK?'

Randy dropped them at an ATM and they drew out the full four hundred to add to the dollars they got in England. Once they settled into their safe house, an ordinary-looking house in a suburban street, they called Lester who, according to the card, was one of their shadows. They told him that they would be going to NASM at eight thirty in the morning.

'You're Jenny, ma'am, is that right? How are you

planning to go there?'

'Yes, I'm Jenny Sorensen. We hoped to get a taxi at eight thirty, if that's likely.'

Lester had a very deep voice and a slow way of talking.

'Well, on a Sunday morning at that time you might have some difficulty. If you don't mind, I know a reliable cabby and I can get him to be at your place that early. Coming back, you should be fine. Not only will it be later in the day, but a lot of cabs operate from NASM. Brad and I will be hovering. We'll be near you all the way. Are either one of you going out today from the house?'

David shook his head at Jenny and made the sign for 'sleeping' with his hands.

'Jet lag, Lester. We can send for a takeout and get some sleep.'

'OK, Jenny. Enjoy your day at the space centre. I'll be seeing ya.'

The refrigerator in the safe house was reasonably well stocked with provisions and two of the kitchen cabinets had tea, coffee and an assortment of tinned foods. However, they both fancied pizza so they phoned out for one Sloppy Giuseppe and one Hawaiian with thin crusts and a large bottle of Coca-Cola. They shared them both, half each.

Next morning the cab came on time and on their way, Jenny came up with a good question for her husband. Bearing in mind that they had never seen or met these so-called 'shadows', how would these guys recognise them as they mingled with the crowds at NASM? The answer was not forthcoming, but little did they know that apart from the intensive CIA training in recognition and surveillance, the two agents were actually three cars back behind their cab which they had followed from the safe house. Both men had photos of the English couple which they had studied and filmed them briefly as they left the house to get into the cab in order to familiarise themselves with what the couple were wearing on this day.

NASM was a huge building complex and when the driver dropped them off near the entrance the queues had already started to form. Many of the people were obvious tourists in groups of their nationality with a leader at the front to take them around. There were families also with the kids tagging along desperate to see the space-age stuff, and not too interested in the early days of flight. Just about everyone had cameras or mobile phones taking pictures of the exhibits and David and Jenny joined in with a group and were listening to the commentary from the guide. Lester and Bradley, the two shadows, had split and were wandering around separately but well within eyesight of their principals. Lester was a six-foot-tall black American in his mid-thirties and had the build of a professional wrestler. He was wearing a thick bomber jacket to keep out the cold and a woollen beanie hat. Bradley, on the other hand, was a normal regular-looking guy dressed in a suit and wearing an overcoat. They were showing as much interest in everything as the others, but their eyes were everywhere.

It was Lester who noticed him first. He was a swarthy-looking older man, maybe in his early sixties, well dressed, but what stood out as unusual was when everyone was looking one way, he seemed to be more interested in something else. Lester kept an eye on him and followed his gaze. At one point he had his mobile on 'video' and was actually filming the group in front of him. Over the babble of mixed conversations around him Lester scratched at his earlobe and spoke into the hidden microphone down his sleeve just below the cuff. Now that Brad was alerted, he too was watching the man from a different position. 'Cameraman' tried to look inconspicuous but to the trained eyes of the agents they knew he was more interested in people than the exhibits. Brad slowly managed to edge his position closer to him in the hope of seeing what he was filming. Suddenly he held his phone out about eighteen inches away from him and took several pictures of something in front of him. Brad pushed forward slightly and got behind him just in time to see the screen of his mobile with a clear image of David and Jenny as they stared up towards a plane suspended from the ceiling. Within a few minutes, cameraman cut away from the group and sat on a bench against one of the walls. Lester ambled round the group and stood not far from the guy making a big pretence of removing his bomber jacket and folding it across his arm as if he was now too warm. His plan was to snatch the mobile and grip the suspect hard but suddenly he realised that the guy had already e-mailed the images to someone.

Cameraman stuffed the mobile into his coat pocket and headed for the nearest exit. Once out of the building he broke into a steady jog and headed for the car park. Many cars all lined up neatly like soldiers on parade, were parked both alphabetically and numerically. He headed down the rows until he came to G4 and removed a remote fob from his coat. The four orange indicators on a BMW saloon flashed twice and he swiftly approached it. As he opened the driver's door, he felt a sharp sting just below his right ear as the needle went in followed by a heavy push which sent him flying across the front seats of the car. A powerful force held him down as he struggled wildly to free himself, his legs thrashing about and sticking out of the driver's door until slowly he felt a wave of tiredness filling his being and he lost consciousness, with Lester lying on top of him and holding his head firmly in his hands. Brad stood next to the door with his back to the car looking around for possible witnesses, but it was too early for anyone to be returning to the car park. Finally, he wandered off and some minutes later he drove up to the rear of the BMW in his Volvo estate and got out with a dark-coloured blanket in his hands. Very quickly Lester wrapped the unconscious body up and placed it in the boot of the Volvo like a bundle of washing. He checked the inside of the BMW but it was sterile, so he locked it with the fob which he then placed into the Volvo's glove compartment. Lester had taken the man's mobile and sitting in the car he briefly checked the photo album.

'He's got nine stills of the Sorensens and about fourteen seconds of video of them,' Brad reported the event to Langley and keeping the mobile phone for further analysis, he drove away. Lester returned to the museum to catch up quickly with the two Brits who were innocently enjoying their second day in the USA completely oblivious of the drama that had just taken place because of them.

CHAPTER 25

As daylight broke over the region and the first fingers of sunshine spread into the compound, a Land Cruiser pulled out through the heavy iron gate and turned onto the dirt road and out of town. There were three men in the vehicle, all grim faced and heavily armed.

The Land Cruiser headed north, with a dust cloud in its wake, to an area called Kujarat some twenty miles from the main township.

They drove past a scattering of roughly made, insignificant-looking dwellings, a very small village of sorts, known for nothing except a runway for light aircraft. Two planes were parked off the strip, one had twin engines and the other was an older single-engine biplane. By now the sun was bright and the men stopped at the far end of the runway. They lit up their cigarettes and silently searched the sky for the plane they had come to meet.

They waited for over one hour but finally a small aircraft came into view with the sun high behind it. When it landed just one man climbed out before it turned around to taxi to the far end where there was a fuel-storage building. The passenger was a heavily built Arab with a thick rough beard and wearing a white thawb. The three men greeted him and appeared respectful as they placed his case into the boot area and helped him into the front seat of the vehicle. He found the journey uncomfortable as they drove at speed over the rugged track, but they eventually reached the main township before branching off down the dirt road towards the big house that stood alone.

Once inside the compound the men showed the visitor into the house where Osama greeted him warmly. They sat and drank strong Arabic tea together before the visitor was shown to a small room on the first floor.

It was his first and only visit to this place. Incognito and using a false passport he had been travelling for what felt like days to get here and he was tired.

In his room was a thin mattress on the floor and lying upon it he rested for over two hours. When he awoke, he lay quietly for a while contemplating, yet once again, his audacious plan. If the destruction of the twin towers made America sit up the way it did and take them seriously, then maybe the destruction of three more towers would make Europe do the same. Right now, it was time for prayer so getting up, he joined the others for worship.

Later, after they had all eaten, the visitor joined Osama in a separate room to talk business and to reveal his incredible plan. From his case he removed three photographs and laid them on the table before Osama. One was of the Eiffel Tower in Paris, the second was the leaning Tower at Pisa and lastly, the Big Ben tower at the House of Commons in London.

'All three should fall on the same day. It will be a technological master stroke and the Iranian brothers are helping us with the details. It would be yet another great triumph for our cause.'

The visitor looked pleased with himself and Osama smiled thinly as he nodded his approval before asking, 'Are there many problems achieving this successfully?'

'Yes, but nothing that cannot be overcome. We could be ready in about two months.'

They continued to talk animatedly for some time and then silence fell across the room. The thin smile had now gone from Osama's tired face to be replaced by a scowl.

'Then let this great deed be done. Allah is with you, my brother, and you have my blessing.'

CHAPTER 26

'Did you have a good weekend?' Frank Bulducci beamed at them from behind his desk.

'Oh yes, thank you. David and I went to the NASM and really enjoyed it. It was very well presented and interesting.'

'Good, good. Uneventful, was it?'

'Yes, absolutely,' answered David. 'We've only been here two days. I should hope it was uneventful, wouldn't you?'

'Yes, of course, Dave. You're right. I am just concerned that your safety is never in jeopardy, that's all.' Behind Frank's smile was the unsettling knowledge that somehow, someone was on to the Sorensens' presence on US soil already. A rat in immigration? Surely not. But then anything is possible. *Shit!* he thought to himself. *It was about six years ago for Chrissake! How can the bastards be that good?*

It wasn't that he was desperately worried about the loss of two Brits on his watch, but if this Sorensen feller turned out to be as good as Casey reckoned him to be, then Frank wanted a result first, before any jihadist action could end the whole project before it even began. It had been a long, hard struggle and his little department was no closer to a satisfactory end now, than they were years ago. For a few days, at least, he would double the watch. It now had to be a full twenty-four-seven job. Hopefully this project shouldn't take too long and the agents could resume normal duties after the Brits had gone home, as he hoped they would.

Although, having thought about it, Frank did consider the usefulness of this Englishman on other CIA projects in the future.

A Failed Attempt

It was not quite déjà vu for them, as they both had expected, thinking back to the pseudo bedroom of the FBI. This room was more like a lounge with an en suite attached. There were two large settees, a couple of armchairs and a desk in the corner with an attractive lamp on it. It appeared that this was not intended for overnight stays, but maybe for civilised interrogations, interviews or just as a rest room. Jenny suspected that the large wall mirror, although fitting in perfectly with the decor, had another purpose and that anyone in the adjoining room, could see, hear and record whatever took place in the lounge.

Frank beckoned them to take a seat. Coffee was brought in by a young girl and placed on the desk and when she left, Frank started the conversation.

'I believe you don't have to be in sleep mode to go into your particular experience. Am I right in that assumption?'

He was right, but David wondered how he knew that, because in the past when the guiding eyes closed down or disappeared, David was somewhat exhausted and wanted sleep. Hence the evening experiments with JD in Washington. However, this was very much the morning and going to sleep was hardly appropriate.

'I don't know why, but the experience inside the eyes seems to leave me drained. A depletion of natural energy if you can understand that. However, if Jenny wakes me fully in a controlled and gentle way then I can carry on with my normal daily activities, after some five or ten minutes' rest, feeling charged up again. What I cannot do, because I don't have that much control in the whole affair, is to lose the contact and then expect it to come back immediately at my demand just because it happens to be convenient.'

'OK, I've got that. Is this set-up here with this room OK for you to drift off, or whatever it is you do?' Frank queried. David nodded his approval.

'If you don't mind, can you please just close the vertical blinds to block out some of the direct light? That then should be fine.'

He had brought with him, more as an experiment, a black cloth about the size of a tea towel. He sat back and made himself comfortable lying askew on one of the settees with his legs stretched out on the carpet. Taking the black cloth, he casually laid it over his face and the top of his head. It looked a little ridiculous, but it did give him a feeling of detachment from the surroundings and within a couple of minutes his breathing had become noticeably deeper and slower. Frank was seated in an armchair with his chin resting in his right hand. His penetrating glare fixed upon David. This was, after all, the first time he had ever witnessed such a phenomenon of this nature, let alone actually being in charge of one. Jenny looked across at him. 'His voice will sound very soft, rather distant. You may wish to get a little closer to him,' she suggested.

He nodded and silently dragged his chair to within a couple of paces of the recumbent figure on the settee. He watched as David's head turned slowly from side to side beneath the cloth as if he was looking around the room. Rather quietly he seemed to be clearing his throat with a soft rasping sound.

'I am in, now. I am in. There is much to see here

and not as I anticipated.' There was a long pause and he stayed very still.

'Forget caves and mountains. This is the site of a large house in a big compound which is surrounded by high walls. I am in this compound now and believe me these walls are twelve feet high. One wall at the far end looks even higher, maybe eighteen feet. This house has been built with total seclusion in mind. There are some chickens and a couple of goats that I can see. They are in this yard. This has got to be where he lives, that is why I am here.'

David went quiet and there was at least a minute of total silence in the room. Jenny was impressed that Frank did not attempt to interrupt the message even though he must have been dying to ask a load of questions and speed things along.

'There is a woman in the yard. She is sweeping an area outside a door that leads into an annexe near the main house. She looks Arabic. I am going into the house now to see if I can locate the man.' Again, there was a long pause of about two or three agonising minutes while they waited for David to report back to them. Finally, he spoke.

'Good God! I am in the room with him. There is no mistaking Osama Bin Laden, but he does look older than I imagined him to be from his picture. He has a visitor with him. An Arab man whom I don't know. They are talking very earnestly together.' David went silent again.

'Location. Jenny. Get him to work on the location, will you?' Frank asked tersely.

She spoke softly near her husband's face, but he seemed to ignore the request for the time being.

'This man who talks with OBL is somehow important. He is showing OBL some photographs with great enthusiasm. I can see them clearly on the table. Eiffel Tower, Big Ben and Leaning Tower of Pisa. I don't know what they mean but they are definitely discussing those pictures. It's all coming from this visitor. I don't understand their language, obviously.'

JD's eyes opened wide. 'My God. Surely not. He cannot be serious,' he whispered to himself, but Jenny heard him.

'David. Can you describe this visitor to me?' she coaxed.

'Stocky build, heavy features. He has thick lips and bushy eyebrows. He is wearing a watch on his right wrist, maybe left-handed, I can't tell for sure. He looks to be late forties. He is quite a bit shorter than Bin Laden.'

'Jenny, this is important. Can you ask him to work

on the location? We must know where the hell we are.' Frank's voice sounded urgent. Jenny coaxed her husband to go outside the building and try and explore the location.

By using his will power 'the eyes' had always seemed to cooperate with David by giving him unprecedented access to things he wanted to view, but only for a limited time. He did not have total control over the process, for 'the eyes' could easily fade away and disappear for no obvious reason. When there was harmony and an inexplicable energy, David knew that it was possible for him to experience an extra sensory perception of events. Other than that, he could not explain the finer details. When he spoke again his voice was even softer than before, his words were uttered slowly and became further apart.

'Outside… now. Large… compound… Messy.' Then silence.

'What's happening? Why has he stopped?'

'We must wait for him,' replied Jenny. 'Just be patient.'

But David did not speak again. The power had gone and David was just in a sort of twilight zone. The CIA man just sat there and stared without speaking. It was impossible to read what he was thinking. He was not an open book.

Jenny, in her own inimitable way, gently brought her husband out of his drowsy state and gave him a glass of water. He sipped from the glass and looked around the room until Frank eventually said something.

'This planet is a very big place, Dave. Any idea where this large house with the high walls might possibly be located? Which country would be a help.' David felt a hint of sarcasm.

'Not yet, no. But then how long have you, and others, been trying to catch Bin Laden? Certainly since before 9/11, which makes it over a decade. Did you expect the full package this morning at our first attempt? The impossible I can do immediately, but miracles take slightly longer, old chap.' David was very serious when he answered back.

Looking at them both Frank asked, 'OK. If this has got to be done in dribs and drabs, then when will you be ready for another session? I'm trying to be reasonable here and don't want to push too hard.'

'Very well then. How about after lunch, say back here for one thirty?' suggested Jenny.

'I should be ready to go again by then,' David replied but deep inside he felt much less confident than he sounded.

Frank rose to his feet. 'In that case I suggest you

have lunch here in the cafeteria and come back to this room after. It saves having your cover agents traipsing after you as you look for somewhere to eat. Will that be OK?' He didn't wait for confirmation before striding out of the room purposefully.

It appeared that the early afternoon was actually too early for a successful repetition of the phenomenon and it acted as a stern lesson for David by letting him know that this was not some inherent power that he could play with whenever it suited him. Whatever that power was, he now deduced it came through him and not from him. He realised at last the big difference. Although David managed to go into the zone without any trouble, the eyes were a 'No Show.' Neither of them could make out what Frank was thinking when the afternoon session flopped, but he sent them home until the following day, without comment.

The House in Abbottobad

That night David had a feeling of disappointment, and as they both prepared for bed he kept thinking of the day's performance. He had a picture of Osama on his bedside cabinet, which he kept looking at, until he suddenly made a decision.

'Jen. Get the audio recorder out, will you please? I'm determined to give this another go. Back to the old days, eh? Just you and me. Let's give it a try. We don't need to be in front of Bulducci, for goodness' sake. We can do this without him babysitting us. If anything happens tonight, we can take in the recording tomorrow and let him hear it.'

As he totally relaxed the band of light approached him in the usual manner, coming at him at incredible speed then stopping a short distance in front of his face. The eyes were in the light which dimmed a little. They appeared to slowly inch forward, growing a little larger but then they merged, as usual, with his own eyes. Instead of looking at the eyes he seemed to be looking through them. Whenever this happened, he found his vision to be amazingly clear, no matter where he was looking. Except that one time, of course, when he was looking for the Picasso painting and found himself in that tiny space beneath a cabinet drawer. But that was more claustrophobic than anything else. As for now, he was well and truly back at the large house with high walls.

Rather shrewdly he decided to use the valuable time that he had, as short as it was, to go in a vertical direction and attempt to find a location instead of wasting effort looking around the house again.

As he went up maybe forty feet or so he was surprised to see that he was looking at a fairly built-up area of a city. The large house was situated a short distance away from the main streets and was, in fact, at the end of a dirt road. It was daylight and there were cars and motorcycles on the dusty roads, but the people were Indian looking, and the area certainly reminded him of a middle eastern town despite the number of solid built houses. Leaving the house behind him he decided to move forward into the town itself to try and find any signs or posters to indicate where he was. Within half a minute, to his absolute amazement, he came across a very smart official-looking military camp with a large placard in English outside the main gates displaying the fact that this was the Military Academy of Abbottabad. He realised the weird reality that the number one terrorist in the world had been living just a stone's throw away from a prestigious military establishment!

While the power remained with him David went back through the eyes to the big house to confirm its location to the Military Academy.

'There are high steel gates at the entrance to the yard which seem to be firmly shut. No one can possibly see into this place. It is very private and secluded. A man is in the yard now, it's not Bin

Laden, a younger smaller man. He is burning piles of rubbish on a bonfire in the yard. Looks like paperwork, personal stuff and food waste. I guess it saves the intrusion of waste collection. Just a guess.'

His last sentence was very slow and quiet and slurred. Jenny knew instinctively that he had slipped from the zone and into sleep state. The recording, however, had produced explicit information. Next morning, they could hardly wait to give it in to Frank Bulducci for analysis. Not that Abbottabad meant a damn thing to either of them but that was, after all, a job for the CIA and its 'Bin Laden Team' to work on.

When Jenny enthusiastically produced their little voice recorder, and between them they explained what had been discovered, the CIA man did not appear to be too concerned. He made an unrelated telephone call in front of them and kept them waiting for about ten minutes before he finished the call and listened to the recording. Without making any comment he picked up the telephone and called an extension within the building.

'Hi Sue. This is Frank B. Can you pick up a recording from my office for analysis? Run it through our intel and see if it flies, OK?' He hung up and turned to the Sorensens.

'If this latest appears accurate I don't see any point

in you two hanging about here today. I can't see what we could achieve that hasn't been revealed already in that recording. Let the shadows know where you are going and hit the shopping mall, if you like. OK?'

David and Jenny checked out of the building and returned home to the safe house to read, watch a movie on television and generally relax before eating out at a very smart restaurant later that evening. They had made the phone call to the shadows explaining their movements but at no time were they aware of anything or anyone unusual watching them. Such was the nature of good surveillance.

Frank rang them the following day to inform them that their recording appeared useful and would be considered at 'Presidential Level.'

'This may take some time before any action is decided and, if it is, then everything will become Top Secret. Neither you nor I will know what's going on until it's all over. This is now a waiting game. You'll hear from me in due course, so be patient. Good work both of you, even tho' it's freakin' unbelievable!'

The Cover Story

The following morning the Director walked into Frank's office and he was frowning.

'Frank, it will be the president's decision of course but I can see this thing taking off big time. If this happens there will be huge media attention and one question for sure will be, "How did the US find him after so many years?" We can never let the Sorensen story get out or he's a dead man. Look what happened to the poor bastard before. They almost got him. How are we going to answer this question when it comes up?'

Frank chewed on his lower lip and gazed through his office window, lost in his thoughts.

His reply was slow and measured. 'We create a cover story. We say that Bin Laden only ever communicated with his followers through a courier, just the one trusted man, which is quite true anyway. This messenger we only knew as 'the Kuwaiti' and we learned this intel from the various interrogations. Once we traced this courier, we eventually followed him to OBL's hide-out in Pakistan. The Sorensens can never exist. Never heard of them. It's the only way. The CIA still get the credit and the Sorensens slide back into the safe shadows of obscurity. I figure we owe them that much. This could be a win-win for all of us.'

CHAPTER 27

The secret silence and the lengthy apparent inactivity from The White House, right down the chain of command to the military, was almost unbearable. David and Jenny were told to go home and never talk to anyone about what they had discovered, but the long wait and the anticipation was wearing on their nerves. They obviously wondered why there was no news of Bin Laden's capture, but there was nobody to ask. Then one fine day at the start of May 2011, President Obama's televised broadcast was screened around the world and the hazardous work of Team Six of the Navy Seals became history.

For the Sorensens, however, the euphoria was short lived. One day Jenny could hear the distinctive ring tune of her UK iPhone which she always kept charged and handy, as it was their only contact with home. She signalled to David to lower the volume on the television.

'Hello. May I speak to Mrs. Jennifer Sorensen, please?' the English female voice enquired.

'Yes, it's Jenny Sorensen speaking.'

'Mrs. Sorensen, I am Cathy Ringham, the chaplain

at Whiteley Village. It's about your mum Brenda. I am so sorry to tell you that she had a stroke and is currently in Saint Peter's Hospital. I know you are in America and I will keep you posted at every step. I am sorry to say it is not looking too good. She is still unconscious, Jenny. I am so sorry, dear.'

Jenny's eyes welled up with tears and she felt so very lonely and far from home. Unable to control her voice from emotion she handed the phone to David who had heard the news also.

'Thank you, Cathy, for letting us know. I will arrange for our earliest possible flight back to England. As soon as I know our date of departure, I will let you know. If Brenda regains consciousness please tell her that Jenny and I are on our way. Will you do that please?'

'Of course I will,' she replied. Then added, 'I will be praying for her all the way. She is a much-loved member of our little community here.'

The Return to England

Jenny telephoned Frank Bulducci to report the news and to inform him that she and David would be returning to England as soon as possible. He was agreeable to the decision but added cautiously, 'You both need protection. You must seriously consider your personal safety at all times, Jenny. I am satisfied with our arrangement in the States, but you will be exposed once you get back to the UK. There is only one company that I would suggest or recommend, and that is PPS. They are in Britain and work for us on occasion, but they exist outside of the law.'

'What exactly does that mean, Frank? Are they a part of the underworld, the criminal fraternity?'

'Not at all. Every agent is vetted and completely trustworthy. However, for Personal Protection Services to be effective in guarding the lives of their clients against extreme violence or assassination, each man or woman in their organisation can carry a concealed gun at some time when they consider it necessary. As you well know, carrying a gun in the UK is illegal.'

Jenny thought for a moment before asking, 'Is this an American outfit?'

'No, purely British, but it's the only one that we take seriously when it comes to efficient protection. They are not cheap, and you would be paying the bill, but you couldn't hire them without some official recommendation. If you agree to it then I will make the arrangements and they will connect with you when you land at Heathrow. Then it's over to you guys. Until you leave the States, we will continue to protect you.'

'Are you suggesting that this firm should protect us forevermore in the UK? Is this what we have come to?' She sounded exasperated, but the CIA man remained passive.

'No. If you remain in Britain, PPS will know if you are receiving some unwanted attention after a while. If everything looks good, they will soon let you know that they do not consider you to be in danger and their duties can cease. Once we make the contact and vouch for you, they will negotiate directly. I strongly suggest that you take up this offer, Jenny.'

She was puzzled by this sudden interest in security when, for years back in England working with Adam on police cases, there was never any worries in that direction.

'Frank, has something happened recently to make you talk of armed close protection for David and me, or are you just paranoid?'

'We are aware from your terrible experience when last in USA that you had become known and were in danger. Having returned it may be possible that you both could have been recognised by the bad guys. Word could follow you across the pond as you return where, without adequate protection, you would be sitting ducks.'

She didn't need to think twice or even discuss it with David before making up her mind.

'Yes. Go ahead, Frank. Please make the call now because we do not have much time. David is making a flight booking as we speak.'

Things moved very quickly after that. PPS received all relevant information from Frank and the English couple were met at Heathrow as they exited immigration and were introduced to a very competent man who called himself Leo. He was a muscular-looking chap, over six feet tall with very short hair and brown eyes that appeared to take in everything around him. He was their personal agent and would be close to them until further notice. He looked like ex-military and the Sorensens felt secure in his company.

They went straight from the airport to the Foxhills Hotel in Ottershaw, and, dropping off their cases, made their way directly to St. Peter's Hospital. But they were too late. Brenda had passed away without regaining consciousness a couple of hours earlier. This news was very sad for both of them. Jenny was an only child and had always been close to her mother. She fell into a settee in the hospital reception and sobbed loudly. As David held his wife tightly and tried to console her, he remembered back to how Brenda had been more like a mother to him than any mother-in-law could ever have been, and he loved her dearly. This was going to be a huge loss for them both. Brenda was always so caring and gentle and was a great favourite in the Whitely Village community.

There was much to do and the two of them worked together with all the phone calls to complete the arrangements. The church service would, of course, take place in the village where she had so many friends. The cremation would be a private thing at the Leatherhead Crematorium but Jenny arranged for a coach to ferry friends from the village back and forth to the nearby Hilton Hotel for the wake. David gave the eulogy in the old village church as Jenny could not trust her voice to keep strong. The little church was filled with Brenda's friends and every detail of that day went smoothly. For a funeral it was a beautiful event. They decided to stay on at the Foxhills Hotel for a further three more days. They collected Brenda's ashes in a mahogany casket and Jenny scattered them among the roses in the Garden of Remembrance at the rear of the church.

During this time Leo did not crowd them but they were always aware that he was close by and followed them discreetly. David had made an impromptu decision and had booked another cruise, this time to the Caribbean, leaving from Fort Lauderdale. When he informed Leo that they would be returning soon to America, Leo insisted on staying with them right up to the point of departure at Heathrow where he could safely see them enter the first-class check-in.

The bodyguard knew nothing of the Sorensens' story, and he didn't ask either, but he gave them his personal card. Now that they were on the PPS files, they could call him any time when they decided to return to England, and he would be happy to continue with the service.

They had been to a meeting with a London firm of solicitors and accountants to brief them about Brenda's affairs and would leave matters in their hands to deal with the necessary paperwork. As executor, Jenny's signatures would be required, of course, but having got that, the firm could manage the rest. Leo had been told that these clients were important and had a red 'High Risk' tag on their file with the CIA. That's all he needed to know.

They ate in the hotel that evening and retired early to their room. As Jenny busied herself with packing their cases David sat quietly at the desk in their suite, lost in thought. Eventually he spoke up. 'Jen? Come and sit down for a minute please. There's something important I've been thinking about and I really do need your input.'

Jenny stopped packing and sat on the bed near to him. 'Go on. This sounds serious. What's up?'

'Well. This is just an idea for you to consider. We have no children, my brother died years ago and now Brenda has gone. Neither of us has any relatives in England and, except for Adam, none of our friends know anything about the whole paranormal experience. Even Adam is now out of the police so I wouldn't be working with him again. Really, we have no specific reason to remain in the UK, have we? America is open to us and we both enjoyed our time there, didn't we?'

'Except that bit when you got blown up,' she replied sarcastically.

'True, but that could happen anywhere. That event came about by putting the spotlight on bad guys. My question is this. How do you feel about us living in the USA?'

'Do you mean forever?' she queried.

'Well, nothing is forever, is it? We could place our house in Twickenham with an agency on a twelve-month rental contract and buy a place across the pond to see how we get on. If it turns out to be the wrong decision we can always come back, can't we?'

Jenny laid back on the bed and stared at him closely. 'Are you considering working again for Bulducci? Is that what this is all about?' she asked pointedly.

David lowered his gaze and studied the desktop for some seconds before answering her.

'What I have unwittingly got is something that can make a difference. A difference for good. Do you think I should just forget about it? Do you think I could do that, seriously?'

'When this all started with your brother's death it was both exciting and incredible at the same time, but then I could see it had the potential for personal danger. I am worried about you associating with the Big Boys in national security. We are like little fish, David, trying to swim in a big pond filled with sharks. Do you blame me for having serious reservations?'

He walked over and sat on the bed next to her. 'Of course not, and I know that there will always be an element of risk, but that's not the main reason for living in America. We genuinely liked it there and besides, if I was to work with Bulducci or the Bureau I have no intention of working this gift nonstop, plus I will be vetting every job they may offer me. I would assist whichever department required me but only now and again and only jobs that I consider fit and proper. I think we should make more demands and be more in control of how things should go than we did before.'

They talked at length late into the evening and Jenny finally felt more comfortable with the prospect of the move and agreed to a twelve-month trial period after the cruise.

They were booked in for an early departure the following day for their first-class flight to Miami to join the cruise ship at Fort Lauderdale. In company with Leo they went by taxi from Surrey to London, dropped off the final documents with solicitors regarding Brenda's will and then checked in to two rooms at the Dorchester Hotel in the West End.

The following morning was the beginning of a bright day in London. Breakfast was delivered to their rooms, after which David phoned the room next door to check in with Leo that all was well and that they were ready. Cases were packed, tickets and passports safely in their carry-on bags, they phoned down for a porter.

Leo was already out of his room and waiting for them on the landing. The three of them slowly made their way down to the reception desk together where David settled the bill. An elderly man was sitting in an armchair in the reception area reading a newspaper. He looked like a retired major from the Indian Army in the days of the Raj. His greased, dyed black hair was neatly brushed back and his thick, bushy moustache was curled up at the ends.

Dressed immaculately in a cream suit, he appeared to take no notice of the trio as they passed him but looking at his watch he took out his mobile phone and made a call.

He spoke softly and calmly in his native tongue and then, picking up his newspaper once more, he continued to read. Contact had been made. It was now up to others. Leo asked David and Jenny to remain in reception for a minute while he made a quick call to a friend.

As the bodyguard stepped out of the front doors of the hotel, he stood at the top of the steps overlooking Park Lane, his eyes carefully scanning 180 degrees for anything unusual.

Everything looked normal. Traffic was heavy and slow moving in Park Lane, but that was to be expected so close to 9am. He took out his mobile phone and walked down the steps away from the uniformed door man and pressed a speed dial number.

'Scotty? It's me. We will be leaving the hotel any minute. Check-in is from eleven at terminal three, Heathrow. Get there before us and give Departures a thorough visual sweep. When you see us, cover our backs as I take the principals to check-in. Just remember, if there is going to be a drama it will be at Departures. Once they are through security, I will join you and we'll go back to the firm together. Don't forget, Scotty. This is a code red operation so, come armed. See you in a couple of hours, OK?' He checked his watch then waved to the first available black cab that was waiting in a small queue near the hotel entrance. He next went back into reception and reappeared with a bell boy who brought out the Sorensens' cases and loaded them into the cab. Once the luggage was all loaded Leo stood briefly by the main doors and gave the whole area one more visual sweep before disappearing once again inside the entrance to collect his two principals.

David and Jenny climbed into the back of the cab with their small bags and sat on the long seat with Leo sitting opposite them with his back to the driver. The cab then pulled out slowly from the front drive of the Dorchester Hotel and into Park Lane. At the top end of nearby Deanery Street, a young man shut down his mobile phone and slipped it into his jacket pocket. He then put on a black crash helmet and pulling down the darkened visor he climbed onto the back of a powerful Kawasaki motorcycle. The engine was already throbbing and the rider, who sat astride it, had his legs out to support it. The passenger tapped him on the shoulder and the bike pulled away with a deep growl towards Park Lane.

From where he was sitting Leo had a clear view of traffic behind them and what was coming up on either side of them. The cab inched its way towards Hyde Park Corner in the slow-moving traffic. The driver decided to take the short-cut through Hyde Park and, indicating right, he eased into the outside lane. Traffic coming towards them from the opposite direction was very heavy and he had to wait for a gap to appear before he could enter the park through the Queen Elizabeth Gate.

As if from nowhere a powerful blue motorcycle with two up appeared on the nearside of the cab. The bodyguard stiffened, his hand going inside his jacket and resting on the butt of his automatic pistol. He stared hard at the riders, the two men wearing identical full-face helmets with darkened visors, but they didn't appear to be interested at all in the cab.

The passenger had his arms around the driver's waist and both men seemed engrossed in looking to their left for a gap to appear in the traffic.

Leo kept his eyes fixed to their hands, only three feet away from him. Suddenly, the passenger snapped his head round to the right and looked directly into the cab, at the same time his right arm straightened and pointed at the window. The gun, a Ruger 44 Magnum revolver had come from the driver's waist band. It was really too late when Leo saw the weapon in the man's extended hand. Even as he wrenched his automatic from his shoulder holster and was swinging into the aim two quick shots rang out and the cab window shattered inwards. The first round went through his shoulder and the second blew a gaping hole in his throat. He collapsed to the floor of the cab making a frightful gurgling sound as blood bubbled from his open wound and he fought vainly to clear his throat to breathe, his body writhing uncontrollably in its death throes.

David was surprisingly quick off the mark, leaping from his seat towards the door, hoping to open it with such force as to knock over the motorcycle and at the same time screaming to the cab driver, 'Go. Go. Go.' On his knees, his hand just reaching the door handle, two more shots went off through the now missing window and half his head was blown away at almost point-blank range. Jenny, who was wearing an immaculate pale blue suit, was instantly spattered in his blood, her face and hair now brightest red like some grotesque mask. Her mind numb and her hands opening and closing she screamed hysterically, waiting for her turn to come. From inside his jacket the rider pulled out some sort of card covered in a plastic wrapping and threw it into the back of the cab. It landed near Leo's head and became trapped in the spreading pool of blood that flowed towards her feet.

Only a few seconds had passed since she saw the bodyguard whip out that gun from inside his jacket. Only a few seconds had passed, but now two men lay dead at her feet and she wished she could just stop screaming. She did not notice the sudden roar of the motorbike, or its front wheel spectacularly rise into the air as the powerful Kawasaki rocketed into Park Lane and disappear north towards Marble Arch. She was not aware of the irate horns blowing their disapproval at the inconvenient traffic jam. She was quiet now, gently rocking back and forwards, staring down at the white card that floated in a sea of thick red, unable to look at David's still corpse resting on her feet. Her mind had frozen in time and horror, locked in this terrifying scene of carnage. Somewhere in the distance she was aware of the cab driver's shrill voice making a frantic call to police on his mobile phone.

Epilogue

Uniformed Police were first on the scene and, with blue lights flashing, they blocked off the road in both directions with their cars. The woman was extremely distressed, and they led her gently from the taxi to a patrol car where she stayed until an ambulance arrived. Witnesses were sparse and their immediate brief statements were not very helpful. The area was preserved as a crime scene as best as possible for the CID officers. Traffic Officers were soon on the scene also. They cordoned off Park Lane properly and put in diversion signs, but the West End was quickly snarling up.

The first detectives on the scene were Detective Sergeant Doug Hannen and Detective Constable Ray Dobson from West End Central police station. As they initially checked the interior of the taxi Dobson swore and stated that it looked like an abattoir. The ambulance had arrived just before them and they tried to interview the woman from the taxi, but she was too much in a state of shock to make any sense and the ambulance took her off to hospital.

Doug Hannen used his mobile phone to take a

photograph of the white card on the cab floor before forensics arrived when they would bag it up. It was clear to him that the writing on it looked like an eastern language made up of lines, dots and swirls. Once written upon, the card had been laminated. This was peculiar. It seemed that whoever the author was, he didn't want his message to get distorted with a load of blood and brains. He then sent the picture to a colleague at the office with a request to get the words identified and interpreted.

This was to be treated as top priority. Just then, two members of the forensics team arrived, dressed in white paper suits, face masks, goggles and rubber gloves. Ray Dobson was trying to get details from a couple of witnesses but Hannen watched carefully as the forensic team discovered passports and airline tickets for two, but interestingly absolutely no ID for the younger second man. They cautiously moved the man over onto his side and they became aware of the Glock 17 still in his hand. There was no sign that the weapon had been fired, no spent cases to be seen. The team continued carefully with their exacting work. Park Lane had been taped off to all except authorised personnel and traffic had become chaotic, but Hannen didn't care. They had an important job to do.

'Ray? Get on the air and do some checks on the

man and woman, will you? I've got details off their passports here. Second bloke has no ID but he is a shooter. Bloody strange this. They've both been shot from outside the taxi through the nearside passenger window. It's like an assassination of some kind, a pre-paid hit. Driver's no help. First thing he knew was the woman screaming. All he wants is his cab back, cleaned up and repaired. Typical.'

'Hello Dougie. What the hell have we got here, eh? A right bloody mess, if you'll excuse the pun.' It was Alan Spencer, the DI from West End Central just arriving on the scene.

'Hello guvnor. Husband and wife together, tickets and passports for this morning's flight to Miami. Second guy, no ID but carrying a gun. Had it in his right hand, loaded, safety off but not fired by the look of things. The hit came from the nearside window. Good shooting, tap, tap, two rounds each into both men. Didn't touch the woman. Maybe she can help when she recovers from shock later. She looked in a bad way, understandably I'd say.'

'Get uniform to guard her for now,' the DI replied. 'This looks a pro hit to me and they might come after her at the hospital. Anything interesting gone into the exhibits bags?'

'Very odd. Looks like the hit man left a note for us

to see. If not for us, then who is it for?'

'Who the hell are these two, then? Are they important players, or what?' the DI asked.

'Passports say British, computer says "Not Known." Maybe mistaken identity, eh?'

The DI rubbed his chin thoughtfully. 'No, no, no. I don't get that feeling. This looks too planned, mate. They knew who they were hitting, looks like a revolver, no empty shell cases. I'm guessing the big fellow with the Glock was protection for the other guy.'

Just then Hannen's mobile pinged and he looked at the WhatsApp message.

'It's the office. Doc. Gobind is on way, should be here in minutes to certify death, and the funeral directors have been notified regarding the two deceased. Oh, breaking news. Stand by. The translation of the card has been done. The words are in Arabic and say, quote, "The Sword of Islam has destroyed another enemy of Allah. The infidel is dead. God is great. God is all powerful." Unquote.'

The DI shook his head in disbelief. 'Oh, for Christ's sake! This is going to be a right uphill struggle, Dougie, if all we've got is a load of jihadist bullshit! Where do you start with that, eh? Anyway, as soon as the bodies are removed get the taxi onto a trailer and into the nick for forensics, although I doubt if much will come from inside. Don't forget to fingerprint both stiffs, especially the younger guy with no ID. I'm going back to the office to contact American police and FBI. Maybe someone over there can shed some light on this mess and tell us why these two should be on a jihadist hit list just prior to going to the USA.'

As he walked towards his car, he lit up a cigarette and then, as an afterthought, he turned back to his colleague. 'Dougie, there's just one more thing, mate,' he shouted. 'Try and get Park Lane open pronto, will you? It's a bloody nightmare past the barriers!'

THE END

ABOUT THE AUTHOR

Michael Till served in the Middle East and Far East as a soldier in the British Army before joining the Metropolitan Police. He served as a uniformed officer in various parts of London before retiring after thirty years' service. He and his wife Gillian now live in a peaceful village in south Devon where they enjoy the beautiful countryside and walks by the coast.

Printed in Great Britain
by Amazon